Murder for Beauty

Murder for Beauty

BEATRICE FAIRBANKS CAYZER

iUniverse, Inc.
Bloomington

MURDER FOR BEAUTY

iUniverse books may be ordered through booksellers or by contacting:

iUniverse
1663 Liberty Drive
Bloomington, IN 47403
www.iuniverse.com
1-800-Authors (1-800-288-4677)

ISBN: 978-1-4620-4314-9 (sc)
ISBN: 978-1-4620-4315-6 (ebk)

Printed in the United States of America

iUniverse rev. date: 10/29/2011

This book is dedicated to
Mrs. Alexander Haig,
who nurtured her husband with love and great input over the years he was an outstanding
Head of Nato , US Army General, and Secretary of State.

Chapter 1

My wonderful wife Hillary, aka Happy, has never before condoned the death penalty. However my huge-hearted Happy changed her mind after the recent horrific murders committed by a serial killer who is beyond all pity.

My name is Rick Harrow. I am a British trainer of racehorses. My wife Happy, a licensed jockey, helps me in my business but moonlights as a sleuth. She has exposed nine serial killers, who had dealt havoc on three continents.

We travel a lot because racehorses go where the races will suit them and the purses are worthwhile.

In my racing career I have won the Arkansas Derby for opera star Fran Purcell Cabrach, and the Dubai Emirates Cup for Canadian tycoon Hal Murphy, plus a race on Arc de Triomphe Day at LONGCHAMPS for French vineyards millionairess Giselle Pont among smaller triumphs on English racecourses for various of my less famous owners.

Yet my minor stable has ever-increasing financial difficulties. I haven't enough owners, nor good enough winners to support the gallops, pay the stable lads, the vets, and cover our own thatched cottage's expenses.

Happy and I are at the beck and call of my most demanding owner, Fran Purcell, now Countess Cabrach as her husband Jeremy inherited castle and title last year when his uncle died. Jeremy's uncle, the late Earl of Cabrach, had sold off the lands around his castle and left his heir no money to maintain the rundown castle. Jeremy, formerly with MI5, had gone to The City to try to make ends meet but also to relieve severe symptoms of a rich-wife complaint.

Fran, who earned millions for her Rap albums that had overshadowed her opera successes, was a pennypincher of mammoth proportions and never offered to help Jeremy to save his castle or me to save my stable. When Fran calls, I answer, and promptly. I hate her pennypinching, her abysmal four letter words, and her adulterous liaisons.

We'd been exposed to her many lovers prior to her marriage: such as the guitarist Goofy, Clearwater's slimy Sherrill, and Sir Arthur Snodgrass. It was her adulterous boyfriends like Bruno the Romanian tenor, the fake Marquis de Talleyrand and one of the serial killers unmasked by Happy, who really went beyond the pale.

"Fuck you, Rick. Sitting on your ass there in Epsom when my fillies could be racing where the sun shines," Fran cursed down the blower to me one February evening when I WAS POURING OVER MY WORRYING LEDGERS IN OUR TACK ROOM. "I'm going to find another trainer if you don't hurry up and get my fillies in some decent races. I'VE BEEN DOING YOUR WORK FOR YOU, YOU BUGGER. AND SELECTED THREE MONEY EARNERS AT GULFSTEAM RACECOURSE IN MIAMI. You'd better get your ass over there, and fast. Or I'll send my fillies there with another trainer."

Very quickly I used Google to study the Gulfstream races, found several that were suitable, and returned Fran's call with an affirmative one of my own.

Within days I had Happy and our three children on a British Airways flight direct to Miami from Heathrow. Meanwhile I'd learned that Fran had two additional reasons for wanting us to go to Florida. She'd got a contract to sing the Musetta role in LA BOHEME at the Kravis Center in West Palm Beach, and was hooked up with a gigolo called Saul Parker in Palm Beach.

Happy and I had expected the temperature to be warm in Palm Beach. But we arrived there for a month's stay during mid-February, when it was as chilly as my own Epsom. Fran, insisting that we rent a bungalow on one of Palm Beach's unfashionable sidestreets, wanted us within shouting distance.

For herself, pennypinching Fran had found a bargain rental in the shape of a huge mansion overlooking Lake Worth that was known to be infested with rats. No comment. Fran had figured she wouldn't be home much, planning to share Saul's apartment overlooking the beach on South Ocean Boulevard.

No mansion for us. As always, I'd brought my wonderful wife Happy with me to help with my string. There are always difficulties when you transpsort highstrung horses from one continent to another, one climate to another, changing the taste and quality of the water and hay. Happy talks to our string, calms the horses and jollies them along to accept the very different turf, the running anticlockwise to our British clockwise and the new grooms.

Happy had looked forward to a hiatus from murders during our Florida sojourn.

That was not to be. She was unpacking our gear and the mountain of children's clothes she brought for our "chillun," when our doorbell gave with its Fifties' style chimes.

Happy, carrying a pile of diapers for baby Richard, went to answer their call and peered through a peephole to see who was ringing our bell. I followed her.

On the other side of the door was a good-looking middle aged woman, who kept her finger insistently on the bell. "I smell coffee brewing" she yodeled through the door's grill, in way of introduction. "Can you spare a cup? I'm your next door neighbor."

Pulling open the door Happy took a closer look at our new neighbor and saw that she was probably pushing fifty. Clever makeup, and maybe one or more expensive facelifts had led her to assume she was thirty.

There was no nearby house. The closest mansion was a Spanish-style pile that reared its tower from behind two-storey-high hedges. Why was this grandiose mansion in our down market neighborhood, did it have rats too? Or was this neighbor seriously wealthy and preferred to live in Palm Beach's oldest section? With her, possibly cachet counts.

"Hello, I'm Merrily Gold, and I really meant it that I need a cup of coffee. My cook has quit, and I don't know how to get our coffeemaker to produce."

The woman had barely entered our tiny hallway when Happy plunked down on its only chair, staring at her as if Saint Peter had just left heaven's Pearly Gates and entered our space.

"Merrily Gold? THE Merrily Gold?" she choked out.

"Yes, dear. And I see you're wearing my WOW!Me Mark IV lipstick." She continued on into the kitchen through its open door, following the scent of coffee.

I wouldn't have recognized the name Merrily Gold, except that last Christmas it had been on a list of cosmetics that Happy wanted under our tree. Yes, our neighbor WAS seriously wealthy. The company that bore that name had cornered the market for teenagers and young marrieds as regarded lipsticks, blushers, mascara, and such.

Happy used all those, and more. Lipliners, pressed powder, foundation, and sun block.

She'd even tried to get me to use the WOW!Me aftershave. No thanks. My favorite smell is and always will be clean horse.

Happy, unsteady on her feet, left the hall chair to start serving coffee. At home in Epsom our coffee was filthy, she tried to filter the real thing. Absolute disaster. Here, in America, I'd already bought Nescafe', the instant stuff, and that was what my darling wife had prepared for the two of us.

To introduce herself further, and perhaps endear herself to my Kentucky-born Happy, Merrily suddenly said, "I recognize your Southern accent. I'm Alabama-born. Did you know that?"

Happy shook her head. Twice. "No Ma'am, Ah sho didn't. Ah's from Kentucky. THET's North o' the Mason Dixon line."

Merrily helped herself to the readied cup that was inscribed: TIM'S CUP. Happy handed me hers that said: MOM'S. I had to wait while she reached into a cupboard and brought out DOROTHY'S to spoon in Nescafe' and boiling water.

Done. The three of us perched on stools alongside a short counter that we usually used to feed the "chillun" their supper. Merrily dug a manicured hand into a box of Ginger Snaps that I'd bought for myself. Happy's preferred bag of cheesebix was still sealed. She opened it to offer cheesebix to Merrily Gold.

Alabama? Merrily Gold, with her preppy New York accent was from Alabama? I racked my brains to recall what I knew about Alabama. "Seventh largest state. A state that still has the death penalty. That is done by electrocution. And in an electric chair with the local nickname: the Yellow Mama."

"Y'all own thet big place beyond them hedges?" Happy asked between sips of coffee. She felt so distracted she'd burned her tongue on the coffee.

"Yes. For about eight years now. But I'm only here for the height of the Season. I go to Georgia next for the PGA Masters. Get some publicity for that. Then to London for the Chelsea Flower Show. At that I was photographed next to The Queen last year. Paris, for the couturier shows. Hate them, because so many of those new designers are bringing out their own lipsticks and perfume."

I interrupted. "Do you return to England for Royal Ascot Races?"

"Of course. Invariably I'm photographed at the entrance. My PR Department makes sure I have a dazzling outfit, I can't be outshone by the likes of Joan Collins! Why do you ask? Any specific reason?"

"I train racehorses in England. Send the best to compete at Royal Ascot. Are you interested in racehorses?"

"Could be. I recall that one of the first great women in cosmetics, Elizabeth Arden, was a devotee of horseraces. Won some good ones." Merrily left her stool, went to the stove, poured boiling water over a spoonful of Nescafe' for another cup of coffee, and then settled back for more talk. Lonely? Had she really come for coffee or did she need companionship?

I pressed on about my string. God knows I'm desperate for new owners, having lost Fanny and Bruce this year, Lloyds' Names, when they went broke. Carefully, very carefully, I edged in:"Would you like to see a video of my stable?"

"Sure. Here? In your kitchen?" She peered around its tiny space to find a TV.

Happy, guessing my game, purred: "Other room. Parlor. We'uns got us a DVD."

She tried to unglue Merrily from her stool. Merrily wasn't leaving the kitchen until she'd reached for the packet of cheesebix, opened it, and grabbed a handful.

It took some minutes for me to locate the best video of our Epsom stables.

Happy doused the living room lights, gentled a cushion behind Merrily's spine where our guest had settled on the chintz-covered love seat, and the DVD flashed its story on the mid-sized 42" screen.

It's a good video. Our horses looked smashing, photographed last autumn before they'd grown their wooly winter coats. Admiral's Barge, a constant winner, tossed his mane and danced on his toes. Hal's Comet put on a show of prancing hoofs. Our filmmaker had provided an excellent background of stirring music.

Merrily wasn't curious about the horses nor the music. She wanted to know WHO owned the horses. WHO was she likely to rub shoulders with at racecourses, get friendly with?

Ah, the loneliness factor.

I reeled off the names of those who were well known beyond my line of country. "Fran Purcell, Countess Cabrach, considered by some as the world's greatest contralto. Prince Mohammed Ben Saud, quite the international playboy, owns a large territory in Saudi Arabia. Giselle Pont, doyenne of prime vineyards in France." I hoped they sounded attractive.

"Fran Cabrach. I know her. Met her the other night at a party down the street. Hasn't she rented the Logan property?"

Happy answered. "Don't know them names of folks on the street. Big house. On Seaview Avenue."

"I'm sure I've been there. Has rats. No exterminator can get rid of them. Goes cheap."

Merrily squirmed against her cushion. "Which of those horses in your video belong to Fran? No winners? She's too tightfisted to pay for good horseflesh."

Carefully, again very carefully, I came to Fran's defense. "The Cabrachs have wonderful winners. She's openhanded when it comes to buying future favorites. I won the Arkansas Derby for her, plus races in Paris and at Royal Ascot."

"What about Dubai? Isn't that where the largest purses go to winners?"

"Yes. And I've delivered in Dubai too. Fran has know-how for good fillies. I've managed to find several wonders for her. And my darling wife has a knack of keeping them at the top of their form."

"Nah. It be y'all wut make the magic," Happy took Merrily's newly empty mug to the kitchen for a third refill. She thought: "Thet there woman ain't goin' to sleep much t'night."

I was pitching my trainer job to Merrily when our eldest boy, Timmy, burst into the living room, squalling: "Who be drinkin' from my cup? Ah seen my Mom fillin' it with coffee!"

Diplomatically, I grabbed the cup from Happy when she emerged from the kitchen. "I've been drinking from it, Tim. Sorry. Here, you can have your milk in mine, that says DAD." I hated to lie to the boy. Both Happy and I were over-conscientious where Tim was concerned, ever since he'd been kidnapped two years ago.

He'd been taken from his playschool in Kentucky while we were on our first trip to Miami, for the horse sales. Miami isn't lucky for us. Last year I'd been accused of killing a boy's father while we celebrated Christmas in a bungalow there. Earlier this year I'd almost had a $4 million horse die on me, until we moved him to Delray Beach. Miami being considered bad luck, I'd welcomed the idea of staying in Palm Beach while our stable's stars performed at Gulfstream.

Merrily shook herself free of the love seat, stood up, and headed for our bolted front door. Earlier she'd preferred the back entrance that led to our kitchen. No 1950's chimes for our slightly larger front door: It had a bark like a Model-T Ford's horn.

I didn't want Merrily to go off without my finishing the trainer pitch. In an overly-personal manner I grabbed her right elbow and suggested I walk her home.

"No need," she gushed, but looked pleased at the idea. I unbolted the door, waited cavalier-fashion for her to exit first, and turned to wink at Happy.

She'd understood the wink meant I needed more time to try to get Merrily into our stable. Happy bolted the door behind us, applied herself to Timmy's needs, polishing the DAD cup so he wouldn't find any trace of coffee in it.

Dorothy and our youngest, Richard, were toddling around the kitchen, playing at an infants' version of hide 'n seek. Timmy wanted no part of that. Sniffing, he went to the 1980's fridge to scour for anything that resembled food from McDonald's. His all-time everywhere favorite eatery, we'd taken him to McDonald's in Russia, Egypt, and France.

Happy always tried to tuck a McDonald's Big Mac or milk shake in our fridges for him.

Chapter 2

Merrily had discovered a gap in her towering hedges that permitted easy access to our miniature garden. I released her elbow as she ducked under the ficus branches, followed her and reclaimed that elbow. "Any chance you'd like to have a horse in my stable?" I put to her bluntly.

Usually I built up a more solid foundation before making the pitch. But I'd shown her a part of our sales video. She'd sat quietly enough. Now I reckoned I might never see her again so it was now or forget it.

"Maybe." She fluttered her WOW!Me-enhanced eyelashes at me. "But why don't you come into my house where we can talk more privately?"

This lady had been in business a long time, I guessed. She knew how to handle requests.

"Sure," I agreed lamely.

During the seven years of our very active and fulfilling lovelife, Happy had only twice had to complain that I'd been unfaithful. Both times she'd been heavily pregnant, and after weeks of sexual starvation on each occasion I'd fallen for a quasi-professional woman who had seduced me. Not the other way around. But I'd never NEVER been guilty of offering sexual favors to female owners or prospective owners. Now, I couldn't if I'd wanted to.

Some months earlier I'd experienced my initial bout of ED.

I'd hoped that it would be the first and only Erectile Disfunction I'd endure. No, when winter opened its icy jaws in Epsom, I'd succumbed to permanent Erectile Disfunction. Had I hoped that a move to fabled Florida might help? You bet! No luck. So we'd tried a short cruise to Nassau, leaving the two youngest "chillun" with a nanny but accompanied by Tim, as usual, who'd had his own stateroom. I'd been fooled by the cruise Ads that bellowed: IT'S BETTER IN THE BAHAMAS.

No sex in Nassau, nor on board the "S.S.Jolly Roger." Not jolly for my roger.

Happy had made light of my agony. She never complained or made snide remarks. It can't have been great for her: God knows Happy enjoys sex, with noisy orgasms and blissful "thankees" afterwards.

She's only twenty-five, and has a long life ahead of her that hasn't any promise of orgasms with her legally wedded husband.

Merrily was flirting with the wrong man as we entered her empty home. I saw no servants on duty. Merrily had one surly butler who was sloppily wearing a T-shirt and jeans. He barely acknowledged that Merrily had come home. No "Good morning, madam," or such. He lopped off to the lake trail.

She enticed me upstairs to her bedroom by alleging that her checkbook was in a desk there and that she wanted to write out the sum of two hundred thousand dollars as a downpayment for a colt she would place in my stable. I was to buy it in the Miami sales.

Today, if possible.

Great! Maybe. Could I hope to find a decent colt on such short notice?

She did write out the check and also signed a contract to enter my stable. No activity on her bed, though.

Not due to my ED.

Her bed, like every available space in every room and the upstairs hall. was totally covered in cosmetic samples. Coming down the hall I'd looked into other rooms and had noted the crowding in each of hundreds of boxes of samples. I hadn't expected to see worse in her bedroom. AND ON HER BED!

There was positively no space for a man in her bed. Crates of the samples packed her coverlet, avalanched from her pillows, and snuck in messy columns down to the floor.

Next to the bedside table there was a space five feet six by eight inches that provided a sleeping area for Merrily.

I thought: That's one woman who's totally obsessed by her business. I said: "Sorry to make this a short visit, but if I'm to arrive in Miami in time for the morning sales, I need to leave now."

Planning my get-away, I slipped on one carton and sent another flying toward her closet.

Merrily's face crumpled. No come-on smile now! She barked: "Damn, you've mixed up the boxes. There's one I positively have to return to my head office."

"Sorry, sorry." I recuperated the carton I'd sent toward the closet.

She tore the carton out of my hands. "That's the one. A damn fool, pushy idiot called Taylor Mead wants me to add some cocaine to my lipsticks. Get the customers addicted. The cocaine-enriched WOW!Me lipsticks are in this carton."

Cradling the carton like a beloved baby, Merrily placed it against the door to her bedroom. She growled, "I always remember to deal with whatever I put here."

Spit wet her lips.

Taking care not to trip again, I inched out to the hallway and, waving a polite goodbye, hurried home.

Chapter 3

I found Happy in the kitchen feeding our two youngest. Timmy glowered nearby, tapping a foot, and preparing HIS pitch to go to McDonald's. After a meaningful kiss, I said to Happy: "Our neighbor gave me a check for $200,000 to spend on a colt. And signed a contract I wrote out to be in our stable. Hooray!"

Happy gave me one of her moon-on-its-back tender smiles, but didn't comment.

To fill her in further, I added: "You should see her place. Downstairs, it's a palace. I believe I spotted a Rembrandt painting in the living room. But upstairs it's a warehouse. Piles upon piles of boxes of cosmetic samples. I tripped on one, and Merrily lost her cool. She told me it contained lipsticks tainted with cocaine. She has some Machiavellian employee in her head office who came up with the idea of hooking customers on WOW!Me lipsticks by adding some cocaine."

"Nah!" Happy left a spoon in a glass jar of applesauce to cross to where a roll of paper towels was tucked in a corner of the counter. She tore off a square of paper and energetically wiped away her WOW!Me lipstick. "Just in case," she explained.

Tim yelled for attention. "Dorothy and Richard don't want no applesauce. They wants to go to McDonald's."

Our eldest is getting more demanding every day.

"Your mother can take you all to McDonald's. I've got to go to the morning sales." I kissed Happy again, pressed thirty dollars into her hand, and rushed for the bus stop outside our front door.

Usually I despised the damn bus. It began at seven a.m. to burp out its carbon monoxide. I'd hear it stop, collect passengers, and then rev up its motor. But we'd rented only one car. And the bus was convenient. It took me to the Fifth Street Station for the Tri-Rail Train. A local shuttle to Miami.

There, I caught a taxi for the horse sales. Entering the premises I greeted some of the American trainers I recognized from my trips to the Breeders Cup races. I went to a stall to buy a catalogue of the horseflesh on offer, and took a stance inside the main arena with pencil in hand to check off likely prospects for Merrily. No second-class colt for her! I knew it was essential to please her by delivering a winner, that could hopefully be followed by others.

While making a note to go see a Nureyev colt, I heard a four letter oath, and turned to stare into the blazing eyes of my richest owner, Fran Purcell, now the very social Lady Cabrach. She tapped my cheek, hard, with HER catalogue.

"You cunt," she swore at me, "sneaking to the horse sales when you thought I'd be busy rehearsing for my Musetta role!"

I rubbed my cheek. "Good morning," I gave with the syrup, not vinegar. "I'm delighted you came to the sales. I hope that means I can buy another filly or two for you."

"So why are you marking the fucking catalogue for a colt when I specialize in fillies?"

She had me there. Rule number eighteen on how to deal with owners: never be negative. "Fran, I'm sorry. Lady Cabrach, shall we go out to view some of the fillies?" I always used her title whenever appropriate.

Fran led like a locomotive with me tagging along as the caboose, to look at several fillies. She pouted, and sneered: "Nothing here up to my standard."

Down went my hopes for one or more new yearlings that would wear blankets in her racing colors. Fran turned to leave the sales and viewing area. She didn't get to the exit. Coming through it were two of her Palm Beach friends: the guy she'd come to Florida to dally with, Saul Parker, who was escorting an exquisite brunette who kissed Fran on both cheeks.

Fran didn't want to introduce me. It wasn't because I was badly dressed: jeans and boots were acceptable here. I guess she'd have preferred I not know her latest lover.

I'd lived through her romancing the previous ones. There had been the musician, Goofy, in London. California had sprung a gigolo I couldn't stand. The most controversial had been Bruno, the Romanian tenor, who might possibly be the father of her baby son. Bruno had been between her sheets only days before Jeremy Cabrach arrived in Milan to hear Fran in AIDA. The day of his arrival was supposed to be the date of conception. Whatever, her little son was now heir to the Cabrach title and castle.

To date, he could pass for a Brit or a Romanian. His stove black-blue eyes could become bluer, his hair could go from hay-blond to raven's wing black. But at the age of three months it was still difficult to be certain who had fathered Peregrine. No one had dared suggest a DNA test.

Fran had been very definitive about her son's paternity. "Darling Jeremy, your son's gorgeous, just like you!" I'd heard Fran repeat in crowded rooms. She had chosen to give her baby that great-uncle's baptismal name, Jeremy having inherited title and castle from Peregrine Cabrach.

The gorgeous brunette introduced herself, while Fran locked arms with Saul Parker.

"Hello, I'm Beryl Blum. And you are Rick Harrow, who trains racehorses."

I warmed to this lovely woman even though she was dressed in yachting clothes, with not a horsehead decoration in sight. Her sculptured black hair swung unfettered by combs or barrettes. She wore a navy blazer with a Yacht Club's coat of arms embroidered on its pocket. A Venetian-gondolier-style T-shirt topped white slacks with a print of sailboats in red. She had needlepoint slippers with her initials flashing. No bling. No jewelry of any kind. I looked for a wedding ring. None to be seen.

Fran was jealous of her: and why not? Beryl, five years younger, with a luscious figure, hadn't needed plastic surgery. Fran, now that her pregnancy was over, had lapsed back into being flat-chested. She'd HAD her nose revamped because she hadn't liked its extravagant length.

Beryl disregarded all the signals sent by Fran telling her to get lost. Opening her Hermes handbag, she removed two large cream colored envelopes.

"Invitations to my ball," she purred. She removed two elegant gold-printed cards that were in the shape of dinner plates accompanied by a silver toned fork and knife set made of heavy cardboard. Very original. "One for you, Fran. And the other for you, Rick."

"May I bring my wife? Her name is Hillary, but she answers to Happy."

"Of course, bring your wife. And here comes my husband. He's had to go to his favorite jeweler to have my rings altered. They were so big I'd have lost them in no time. Livingston, meet Rick Harrow. He trains Fran's racehorses."

Fran stopped pouting. Livingston was all-man, glowing with love for his wife. I could recognize the aura of a husband who enjoys great lovemaking with his mate. Fran looked at him from the viewpoint of a predatory female. I could have told her she was wasting her talents. This man was truly in love with the bride he'd chosen.

"How long have you two been married?" I asked.

"Three months, three weeks and six days," Livingston volunteered.

At the same time, Beryl said: "Four months."

Chapter 4

Their varying replies reminded me that I'd often given thought to how with many couples one partner loves more than the other does.

I queried further, "Are you both in business?"

Nods. Livingston looked slightly abashed. He said, "I'm a lawyer. Partner in a small law firm in New York City. You, uh, you've never heard of Beryl Blum Cosmetics? My wife is THAT Beryl Blum."

What to say to him now? I bit my lower lip, and said nothing. Did Livingston suffer from Rich Wife syndrome?

Beryl turned to Fran. "We're having a few friends aboard the BERYL for lunch. Would you be able to join us?"

"Is Saul invited?"

"Of course. You aren't selling real estate down here in Miami, are you Saul?"

He shook his head.

As an afterthought, not wanting to appear unkind, Beryl added: "And you, Rick, trainer of racehorses. Would you like to come?"

No, I wouldn't. I'd traveled to Miami to look for a colt, not lift cocktails-to-lips on a yacht. I was still without having accomplished my mission, thanks to Fran's dirty trick of pretending she wanted another filly to add to her string, when I now realized she'd come to the sales to stalk Saul.

I bowed my head with the short gesture I usually reserve for my sovereign, and said, "Thank you, Mrs. Blum, but I have to stay on here for the afternoon sales."

"Too bad, You're going to miss some fun. We're starting out at my grandmother's Causeway house."

"Sorry, but I—"

"Europeans get a kick out of her house. There are two islands off the Causeway, Palm Island and Star Island. When my grandmother bought hers, Al Capone lived on the other island."

"That's the Chicago gangster, that was? I recall his brother had some fast horses."

"Yes. My grandmother lived there at the same time. And one day she was invited for tea by Mrs. Capone."

"That must have been something!"

"Yes, it was. My grandmother took her European houseguests to her island. They went to her island. Then to Capone's. They were fascinated, hoping to see a real live gangster pop in from the next island. Tea, was iced tea. As a parlourmaid was bringing in a large silver tray with the glasses, she dropped it with a resounding crash. My grandmother and all her houseguests fled, they thought a mob-style shooting was happening. Are you deetermined you won't come for drinks there, and then go on my yacht?

"Yes. Sorry," I escaped.

That foursome wound out through the exit, chatting about Beryl's ball. I found a bar with a stand-up table where I wolfed down two sandwiches followed by a beer.

Lady luck appeared just before closing time. A really neat colt came up for auction after most of the heavy bidders had left. I looked into his eyes. I found intelligence, honesty, and good will. Would he be fast? I scoured his genealogical background for winning mares. The stallions were first rate. Finally I ran my hands down his legs. They had no heat, and his hooves were sound. I bid for him, there was no opposition. I got him for Merrily's two hundred thousand. A bargain, if he IS fast.

The paper work is always a hassle. But these sales people had endured two long days and were as eager as I was to go home. We accomplished the necessary. Merrily's bank account number, the last four numbers of her social security card, and the zip code of her Palm Beach address 33480 all finalized the business.

I was heading North on the Tri-Rail before sunset.

An hour later when I arrived in West Palm Beach the full flowering of the sunset was in progress. And it was a sublime sunset, true to Florida's reputation for glorious hues in shades of vermilion and mauve. As I crossed the Lake Worth bridge going East toward the four rows of Royal Palms, I looked South and saw that cumulus clouds had been painted vermilion by the sunset and their reflections had turned the lake's waters into the color of a good vin rose'.

The first stars were emerging when I arrived at our little house.

Happy was feeding our three "chillun" AND Merrily. Again! Happy was heating the contents of a can of tomato soup. Merrily had a mug ready. It was my mug, with DAD written on it plainly. A packet of Ritz crackers lay on its side with several crackers spilled on to the counter. Merrily was chomping on a cracker.

"Hiya, Honey. How'd it go? Did y'all get a fine colt?"

"Hello, family." I kissed Happy, and Dorothy, then patted the heads of our two boys. I walked over to Merrily and placed in her ready right hand all the paperwork I'd collected on the colt.

Merrily pulled out her reading glasses from a pocket and, all business, read every word.

For once our kitchen was quiet while our tots munched on Big Macs that Happy had unloaded from a take-home bag. I would have liked a cup of the tomato soup, but knew there wouldn't be enough for three adults and so I wandered to the 1980's fridge and dug out a jar of marmite and piled a healthy glob of it on a slice of whole wheat bread.

Timmy broke the silence. Not satisfied with his own meal, he finished Richard's and Dorothy's mini-sized burgers. He said: "We didn't get any toys at McDonald's. They'd run out of them. What did you bring us from Mi-a-mi?"

Truthfully, I growled, "A good-looking racehorse for Mrs. Gold, here."

"She done brought loads of hern samples," Happy said brightly. "Dorothy and I have had one real ole fashioned Fair Day tryin' out them creams 'n per-fumes."

"That was kind of you, Mrs. Gold," I said. "But how will you ever unload all those many cartons you've got in your house?"

"No problem," Merrily removed her reading glasses, tucked them back in her pocket, and folded the colt's papers. "In Palm Beach there's a charity gala almost every evening. Charity luncheons too. Estee' Lauder launched the idea of distributing samples at charity events. Now everybody in the cosmetics world does that. The trick is to get the samples given out at the top balls: Red Cross, Heart, Cancer, like that. I'll run out of samples before the balls stop."

Balls. I remembered I had an elegant card in my pocket inviting Happy and me to Beryl Blum's ball. I dug in my trousers and delivered the much-creased invitation.

"You might like to go to this, darling."

"Sho nuf. Ain't been to no fancy ball since Milan, when we'uns met Maheen at the ho-tel where she were naked in thet Three Graces purty settin' all covered in fake gold dust."

Merrily pushed out a hand to hold the invitation. Out came the reading glasses. "Beryl Blum!" she shrieked so loud I wondered if the neighbors further down our street could hear. "And this ball's a week from Tuesday, same night as the Carolers' Ball where I'm giving away eight hundred samples of WOW!Me Mark IV."

"Y'all knows Beryl Blum?" Happy asked in awe. If she'd been Dorothy's age she might have been speaking of Santa Claus.

"Certainly. In the cosmetics world all of us know one another. We go to the same conferences, woo the same magazine and newspaper fashion writers, have our counters alongside in the same cosmetics sections of department stores. Beryl Blum! I've always said we should leave out the 'l' from Blum and call her 'that B-word of a Bum.'"

Lamely, I said, "I think she just recently got married. Four months ago. Or so she told me. I guess this will be a sort of delayed wedding reception."

"You guessed wrong. You don't know Beryl Blum. She's the original mountaineer social climber. She's rented a house in Palm Beach to make her mark on the social season. Bought that wimp of a Livingston for her husband. But doesn't use his name. His ancestors came over on the Mayflower, from Plymouth rock. Hers, in steerage, for Ellis Island. Even so, she continues to be known as Blum, because she's so vain about making it so big in such a highly competitive business. Beryl the Bum!"

Happy served the steaming tomato soup. The one can had made enough for two, just as I'd supposed.

Beryl burnt her tongue on the soup. She let out a yelp. I hoped that would be the last we'd hear from her that evening. No, she held on to her seat after pouring cold water from the tap into my DAD mug. She grunted, "I won't be going to her ball. I've already promised to make a personal appearance when my eight hundred bottles are distributed at the Carolers' party at The Breakers."

"Thet sounds like a real nice e-vent," Happy said, trying to calm the feathers of this very agitated lady-bird. SHE wouldn't have forgotten that Merrily had become the new owner we'd so much needed.

"I'll see to it that you get a free ticket, Happy dear. You, Rick, can go to that Beryl person's ball, if that's what you want." Merrily, seeing there was nothing more to eat, stood up and found her own way to the kitchen door. In another minute we heard her swear the F-word as she scratched herself going through our hedge.

As soon as I'd closed our kitchen door, I leaned against it and said regretfully, "Maybe it IS better that you go to Merrily's party. We'll split ourselves into two fawning idiots, each trying to get more horses into the stable with these owners."

After our "chillun" had been bathed and read to, we left them sleeping in their cots and I opened the covers of our kingsize bed. Due to my ongoing ED, I had no illusions that we'd be enjoying sublime sex tonight. The cuddling and kissing would have to do, and that would comfort me.

When we were first married and in heat for sex, Happy wanted a story after we were satiated in bed. I would try to become a male Scherazade. She'd drift off to sleep with her mouth in that delicious moon on its back position.

This night she primed me with questions, her voice awe-tinged, "Wut-all she be like, thet Beryl Bush? Right purty? Full o' hersef? Or she be sweet-like?"

"Pretty, yes. Not quite what I'd rate as beautiful. But her looks are all natural. She uses very little of her own makeup. No snob. Business-orientated. Nice, though. Not as totally absorbed in her business as Merrily is. And I don't agree with Merrily that Beryl's husband married for the money. I could see his eyes were blazing with love for her."

"Fran says them Beauty Queens be Billionaires, not just millionaires. Least-ways them cosmetic companies be worth billions."

"No arguing with that. But darling, are you thinking this Beryl Bush could be a candidate to become one of our owners? Think again. She's totally into yachts."

"Don't know nothin' about no yachts. Just the same, Ah'd sho like to meet her."

Chapter 5

She did.

Fran had given us two tickets for her Dress Rehearsal. She must have received a block of four, because we found ourselves seated next to Beryl Blum and her Livingston.

Lady luck had smiled on Happy: she was knee to knee with Beryl.

The Kravis Center had been built in the 1970s to accommodate rows of seats that were so close that latecomers had to climb over the knees of those seated prior to their arrival. Happy loved feeling the heat from Beryl's outer thigh as it warmed her stocking-free legs.

I introduced my Happy to Beryl and Livingston, who were all smiles.

Livingston had his hands firmly grasped around Beryl's. She kept looking around to enjoy the acclaim that her fame had warranted as members of the audience recognized her and applauded. My glances roamed from the tall pillars topped with a Lotus motif in a bow to AIDA, the first of the many operas given here, and up to the chandelier on the ceiling reminiscent of the one that falls on theatergoers in PHANTOM OF THE OPERA.

I wanted to chat with Beryl, but she was self absorbed. Just before the swish of the First Act's rising curtain Beryl acted politely sorry to learn that Happy would miss her ball. They had just met that evening, but Beryl added, "Nice, that we could come to this Dress Rehearsal together, anyway."

During Intermission, that we call the Interval, Beryl invited us to join her in the Founders Rooms on another floor. "I wasn't a founder. But I DO help many opera houses around the country when they need some financial bailout or other," Beryl explained.

She showed a card to a lurking guardian of these ultra-private facilities, and we were seamlessly admitted to the Founders' premises.

The rooms were superb. Decorated in good taste where the members could feel they were in London,

Paris, or Rome for an evening of Opera, we were pressed to accept flutes of champagne.

Happy preferred the oversized trays of handmade chocolate candies that were a specialty.

Only too soon lights were flicked to announce it was time for the Second Act.

Fran was born for the role of Musetta in LA BOHEME. Fran playing Musetta, a tremendous flirt, took over the stage as she sashayed from man to man in the Second Act's famous restaurant scene. Fran was in good voice. Her natural predatory-female persona emerged in full bloom. Flat-chested she was, but that offered no hindrance when every cell of her body spelled LUST.

This version of LA BOHEME was produced in English, rather than in its original Italian. As Fran completed her great aria WHEN I WALK DOWN THE STREET, the Kravis audience rose to give her a huge ovation.

She received additional plaudits when we returned to Beryl Blum's rented house for after-performance drinks.

Beryl started the plaudits. "You were fantastic! You certainly deserve to be the Guest of Honor tomorrow night when we celebrate your Opening Night."

Chapter 6

"Damn all," in her most celebratory mood, Fran used one of her least offensive four letter words, "Damn, damn, damn, I could have done better. I should have held on longer to that final note. Give me a drink. Got any champagne?"

"Yes. Not chilled, though. Crates of it for tomorrow night. Have a whisky and soda," Livingston quickly produced a heavy cut-glass tumbler filled with ice. He poured a double shot and added very little soda.

Fran gulped down the drink as if she'd been a miner lost in a desert. She said spikily. "I hope it's Moet Chandon for your party tomorrow night."

I smiled, knowing that Fran would never ever produce first class champagne at any of HER parties. Our pennypinching owner usually served Mimosas so that her guest had difficulty recognizing the quality of the champagne she'd mixed with orange juice.

There were only six of us in this group. Our hosts, Fran and her Saul, Happy and I.

Saul had arrived after the rehearsal, giving staccato apologies for his late appearance. "I'm working on selling a lakeside dump for a couple of million. Sucker wouldn't see me earlier."

This gave me ample opportunity to look around Beryl's house. The place was stashed with fabulous antiques. The French Provencal furniture was authentic and updated with the most appropriate tropical-print chintzes. In the library I was astonished to recognize an original Audubon folio of engravings of his watercolors, dating from 1827. I'd seen a similar one photographed when it was sold at auction for $10,270,000, sold by Sotheby's in London to an anonymous buyer.

John James Audubon, born in Haiti, made watercolors of American birds he'd studied in the wild. This folio measured more than 3 feet by 2 feet because Audubon wanted to reproduce the birds lifesize. Collectors hold his works in reverence, as did the absent owner of Beryl's rented house, because he'd positioned a ceiling light to add a glow to the extraordinary colors of its cover.

I used a gesture to point out the home's outstanding treasures. I said, "Livingston, how come the owners of this place didn't put these amazing pieces into a storage facility? Seems incredible they'd leave them to renters."

"Beryl insisted they remain in place. No antiques, no deal. The owners didn't give us a hard time. We only took the house for a month during the height of the season. They wanted to enjoy them on their own before they head to Newport for the summer."

In the main salon there was a magnificent concert-style grand piano. Fran strummed her fingers on its ivories, reprising the melody of Musetta's main aria. Her mood improved with succeeding tumblers of double shots from Livingston's whisky decanter.

I wasn't spying on her, but because Livingston and I were getting better acquainted next to his bar, I couldn't help counting how generous he was with the drinks.

Happy, ecstatic at being in Beryl's home, and chatting with her as if they were longtime buddies, nevertheless was counting Fran's drinks too. Out of compassion for this most difficult of our owners and in the full knowledge that Fran's heavy drinking would badly affect her vocal chords, Happy announced she was ready to end the evening. "Ah's got a babysitter wut Ah's got to pay 'n drive home."

Looking longingly at Livingston's unusual bar, shaped liked a Guignol from a Paris park, she gave up any chance for drinks for herself and led Fran to her limousine. We lived merely three blocks away, but a limo had been ordered because Fran's vocal chords weren't to be exposed too long to the night air. It was still cold outside, unusually bitter for a Palm Beach February. The cold spell had lasted longer than usual.

Obediently, like a child hurried to take the school bus, Fran went to her limo. Grasping Saul's arm, it looked obvious that she had given up the drinks for sex. But Saul didn't dance to Fran's tune. From the parked limousine he walked Fran to her door, then returned to the limo, gave instructions to leave us at our little house, and drove away to his own home. Lady luck had smiled on Fran's opera career. She would have been very hoarse for her Opening Night performance after a night of heated lovemaking with Saul.

Chapter 7

Happy took great pains with the gown she chose for Merrily's charity night.

The Carolers' party wasn't one of the grandest of the Palm Beach season. It drew the B-List, not the A-List. Happy wasn't to know. For her this was a grand occasion and merited a very special dress.

Because we were so short of funds, Happy copied her English friends' custom of raiding the charity shops. She found a pink silk all-beaded gown that needed work because several of its beads were missing. She spent her free time to sew on beads between early morning gallops, the school runs, and evening gallops.

By eight in the evening, with a babysitter installed, and having helped me with knotting my black tie, she scooted through the gap in our hedge to cadge a ride with Merrily to The Breakers. Our house was five blocks from The Breakers Hotel, but it wouldn't have suited Merrily's glamour image to walk up to its entrance.

The last I saw of Happy, she waved grandly to me from the passing limo while I trudged the three blocks to Beryl's South Ocean Boulevard rented mansion.

There were clumps of parking boys lined up a block from the party. As valets, the boys ran forward to take over a driving seat, park the corresponding car, and hook the car's keys on a large placard leaning against the oceanside wall.

I gave a salute to several of these boys, while simultaneously I felt impressed with the size of the tent erected for the ball.

Although it seemed unnecessary to have a tent when the mansion was so large, I could hear voices engaged inside where other guests had arrived more promptly, and people were strolling from one bar to another stationed closer to the house.

I made my way to the gigantic front door, more appropriate for a mosque than a home, and quickly passed through a receiving line that included Beryl, Livingston, and two opera heavies whom I didn't know. Heading for the tent's bars, I noticed that most of the guests hadn't arrived, probably because they'd paid to go to the opening night of La Boheme. There were gaps in every room, with only a few couples chatting in corners.

At ten o'clock a light supper was served in the tent. The early guests understood that the main dinner wouldn't be served until the Guest of Honor appeared after the opera.

On the stroke of midnight, an avalanche of opera buffs poured down the receiving line. No Fran. The din from all their voices was unpleasant, and I returned from the hallway to the tent to wait for Fran's grand entrance.

SHE MADE ONE! Cleverly holding back to remove stage makeup but not her Musetta costume, Fran remained in her dressing room at the Kravis until her perfect moment arrived for her to idle through Beryl's pair of massive doors. Fran knew that would be precisely when partypoopers were complaining that she wasn't going to turn up.

Fran was escorted by a not-very-pleasant Saul. He barely managed to pull his lips into a poor excuse of a smile.

The Musetta costume, made to order, was extremely becoming. Just as she had done in Madrid in her Zarzuela-inspired costume, Fran made use of these props whenever there was a man in her crosshairs.

Standing next to the bar it was easy for me to grab two flutes of champagne planning to press them on to Fran and Saul.

An older woman, a Palm Beacher with several facelifts in her past, raised a flute of her own and yodeled: "To one of the greatest contraltos of all time."

"Hear! Hear!" was shouted from various corners.

The members of a danceband filed into the tent and unpacked their instruments. No music for the earlier buffet supper! Would Fran sing? I doubted it. She'd refused Hal Murphy in Dubai although he'd offered her a fair sum. With her kaleidoscope personality, later in Madrid when Hal's son was going broke because his wrestling match had been stopped, Fran had offered to warble some of her most famous arias as a free entertainment. Fran! I've often thought before, love her or hate her she's sure something!

"I'm famished," she declared on arrival. "Where's the food?

Beryl heard that, and made a big deal of leading her Guest of Honor to be seated at a head table set up in front of a horseshoe arrangement in the vast dining room.

I made to follow the leaders inside, but halfway to the top table our Fran half-turned and called to me: "Bring another two glasses of bubbly."

There was a long queue waiting for drinks at the nearest bar. I crossed the tent to a less popular watering hole on the far side. My second flute of champagne was being poured when we heard the first shrieks of horror.

"Fire! Fire! My hair's on fire! My gown's on fire! Help! Help me! Help! Help!"

Leaving the bar, I rushed toward the dining room beyond the tent's far end. An avalanche of escaping guests thrust from the room, trampling one woman underfoot, and shoving an elderly man to his knees. Among the people in that crush I saw Saul, his hair singed and his dinner jacket smoking. He was busily slapping at two spots that were still burning.

No Fran.

I struggled to keep my footing. Desperate men and women had no thought of anything except to save themselves from flames that were now searing through French doors leading to the tent. A corner of the tent began to spit and smoke.

Was this tent fireproof? I tried to recall whether or not asbestos had been denied to tentmakers. Yet, hadn't many circus tents and wedding reception tents caught fire? There were no exits from this tent except through the French windows to the house. The epicenter of this disaster.

Suddenly a car's wrench tore out a panel that simulated a window. Two valet parking boys were attempting to provide an escape route. The avalanche of people charged in that direction, and one by one a few women and two men ushered through before the flap caught fire. One of the men was Saul.

I grabbed a carafe of water and poured it on my shoulders. I took a dinner napkin, wet it with a bottle of tonic, and pushed against the oncoming tide. Where the flames were thickest no one was attempting to lunge through the farthest French window. I headed for it, and with no other thought than to locate Fran, I rushed inside.

Fran, still alive, was pinned like a butterfly by a fallen chair leg. Struggling to pull free, she could gauge how close the flames were reaching. Like the tentacles of a vermilion octopus the fire leapt from table cover to table cover. Unbelievably it had not come to the top table. I raced toward it, breathing through the napkin like a surgeon into his mask in an operating room. I yanked at the table leg, freed Fran, and pulled her toward the great front door.

Fran, being Fran, resisted me pulling at my arm and beating me with her other fist. "I've got to find Saul," she sobbed.

Once outside on the gravel driveway, where two fire engines had arrived and two firemen were attempting to uncoil hoses, I said: "That rat left the sinking ship in plenty of time. What about Beryl? And Livingston?"

Fran couldn't speak. She shook her head.

Fran's limo driver found us, and led the way to his vehicle. Many other cars had been abandoned by the vast majority of parking boys, but this driver had recognized his keys on the valet board and could recoup his Lincoln.

Finding her voice, Fran finally answered: "Burnt to crisps."

. "Driver," I said, speaking carefully, "Please take Countess Cabrach to her home. I'm going back to that inferno to see if there's anything I can do."

"Rick, you can't leave me alone. I've been to Hell tonight. There will be no one at my house for me. The hired help only come a few hours during the day. Fuck you!"

The Driver swiveled from his front seat, "Police won't let you near that place. Forget it. Where you live, Mister? I'll drop the lady, and then take you wherever."

Oh, Fran! Feeling desperate to rejoin Happy, who would be smelling the smoke and wondering if I'd been caught in the flames, I said to the driver: "Drop me on the corner. You're right, there's not much I could do if they put up barricades. Fran, please understand that I need to calm any fears that Happy may have. See you in the morning."

Before Fran could give with one of her expletives, I took advantage of a red light on Barton Avenue and hopped out of the limo. I watched the limo pull away, with a vignette of Fran shaking a fist at me. There hadn't been a word of thanks for pulling off the chair leg that had pinned her down.

Happy was standing at the gate of our white picket fence, her eyes straining to watch for me through the biting ashes.

Chapter 8

"Thankee dear God, thet y'all be saved," she squirmed past the gate and squeezed me hard. "Ah's let the babysitter go befo'e Ah done seen flames 'N smelled this ac-rid smoke. Couldn't leave ourn chillun alone to go seachin' fo' y'all. How be Fran? Beryl 'n Livingston?"

I shook my head. "I got Fran out. Nothing could be done for Beryl, or her Livingston. I believe they were trapaped in the Library, trying to usher guests to the dining room."

"Daid?"

"Yes. Fran had a piece of wood pinning her down. I came to her in time to get it off her and hurry her outside. Come indoors, my darling. This smoke is deadly."

"Like in thet 9/11 tra-ged-y when tiny bits o' body parts mixed in with the sooty air."

"Something like that." I bolted our kitchen door, closed the open windows and turned on the air-conditioner's fan. It was still cold for Florida, but we needed to have unpolluted air.

"Rick, y'all done ruined thet dinner jacket from the rental place. Both sleeves have burned marks, and the back is still smolderin' from the fire. Wut y'all goin' to tell them folks wut rented it?"

"What I'm telling you. I need to wipe out the whole story from my mind. Let's go upstairs and get some sleep."

Prior to my ED trouble, we could have made love and that would have been the best balm for my agony. Instead, I changed out of my ruined clothes and spreadeagled on our kingsize sheet.

I hoped that sleep would diminish the horror.

Neither of us could slep. Finally, after two hours of tossing, I asked: "Want to tell me about the ball?"

"Weren't much. Cain't hardly remember much after watchin' po'r Beryl's house burnin' down and smellin' all them daid crisped people. Purty dec-o-ra-tions at thet ball. Por-ce-lain Carolers as centerpieces. Ah's esked ifn Ah could have one. Told no, 'cause they wuz fo' dec-o-ra-tion only."

"Food?"

"Nothin' special. Chicken. Guess them or-gan-i-zers wanted t'save money to give to them Carolers. Folks applauded Merrily fo' the take-home presents. She stood up, 'n bowed. Then us'n headed home. Merrily, she were real pleased with thet applause."

Not a great ball."

"Naw. Not without y'all t'dance with. Hold me in yourn arms."

I kissed her, hugged her. About four in the morning I went to sleep. I had nightmares dreaming of partygoers screaming as they were burned to crisps.

Chapter 9

I'd hoped sleep would help.

It didn't.

In the early morning I compounded my misery by accompanying Happy to view Beryl's house. Much of it was still smoking. There were firemen on scene damping away.

We saw mortuary trucks come from the Quattlebaum funeral people who were attempting to individualize body parts for eventual burial. No need for incineration. That had been done. We picked our way around the burned out wrecks of cars abandoned by the parking boys or owners. Happy seemed inordinately interested in that area of the grounds.

"Lookee here," she called to me, while pushing aside the valets' board that had held owners' keys. The board was in fair condition, with merely one grounded corner singed. Its keys were heavily coated in black ash. Happy was pointing behind the board.

I peered at a contraption there, which didn't make sense to me. I saw ordinary pine cones, the sort that fall off trees all over America. These pine cones were coated in candle wax.

Happy retrieved one, and pocketed it.

She whispered: "Back in ourn Kentucky hills, we'uns cover pine cones with ourn candles' melted wax. Sho be proven way to start a mam-moth fire."

I digested her inference. Feeling like Atlas carrying the world on his shoulders, I headed for home to make the obligatory call to Fran.

She was awake. Her four letter words streamed from the receiver: "What the fuck you been waiting for? You're such a shit. I've been phoning you for the last half hour. All I got was some stupid nerdy babysitter. I need you to drive me to the Kravis Center. I'm going to have to try on several costumes for my Musetta role. You're an asshole. You KNOW my costume was ruined last night."

"What time shall I collect you?" I breathed out like a woman in labor attempting to dull her birth pains.

"In an hour. And shit, that means not a moment later." No mention of angst from the fire the night before, nor the horrendous deaths of her two friends being roasted alive.

Happy had taken the morning's newspapers from their plastic sheaths. She was waving the Palm Beach Daily News with the urgency of a XVII Century sailor in a high mast warning of an approaching pirate vessel.

"Lookee at them headlines," she choked. "Worstest fire in this town's hist-o-ry. Such purty picture of Beryl, with loads about her humongous company. Not much about Livingston."

"How many dead? How many hospitalized from burns?"

"Don't rightly say. Seems like sixty-three dead, but one of them badly burned ones may not last out the day, makin' sixty-four. In hospital? One hundred 'n twenty-six. Not all o' them folks be Beryl's guests. One valet, three waiters from the caterin' service. Po'r souls. Just tryin' to make a livin'. Lists them purty paintin's and fine ant-iques wut gone too. Says the owners were self-in-sur-ed. Says like Beryl's es-tate may be sued by the fami-i-lies wut lost loved ones. Tent weren't properly treated agin' fire."

Chapter 10

I sat down. Put my head between my hands. Happy gently placed beside me the thick assortment of sections from The Palm Beach Post. I separated the news section from ACCENT, SPORTS, LOCAL, and BUSINESS.

The front page carried an agonizing picture of the scorched remains of dead bodies laid out on the gravel driveway, with two fire engines in the background surrounded by gaping crowds. God! I felt relieved those crowds had left by this morning. I believe I would have kicked a curiosity-seeker if he'd got too close in my line of sight.

"Please, darling. Don't take our "chillun" to see the ruins of Beryl's house."

"Ah's won't. If y'all goes in the car to fetch Fran, Ah'll stay home and bake cookies fo' them."

Cookies! I've eaten those rock-hard turds in the past. It was no wonder that Timmy and Dorothy preferred Big Macs or CHICKEN McNuggets.

I collected Fran on time. She was huffing and puffing like the wolf in the Hansel and Gretel children's tale.

And whom did I see waiting at Kravis's VALET PARKING ENTRANCE? Saul. Oh God, did I have to put up with him?

Fran explained: "I need his advice which of the costumes on offer I should fucking choose."

Not quite the absolute truth. I knew she hadn't been speaking to Saul ever since he'd abandoned her to the dining room's flames while he escaped via the tent's meager opening. But with Fran, sex was all-important and she hadn't had any for forty-eight hours. With her husband Jeremy still in London, she'd turned back to Saul.

Like soldiers in native-run countries said, "We take what's on offer."

Saul made no excuses for his appalling behavior. He kissed Fran publicly, and the three of us strode to the stars' dressing rooms area. Fran left us to follow a waiting dressmaker, present to make any alterations needed.

Saul winked salaciously at me, and said, "Lucky you, to have a bit of ass at home to have fucked away your memories of the fire."

Dumbly, I groaned, "I have ED."

"Really? Why haven't you used Viagra?"

"Gave me the father of all headaches, and extreme pain in my sinuses. Anyway, doesn't work for me."

"And cialis?"

"I couldn't stop vomiting. Didn't work for me, either."

"Get yourself a prostitute. Not a young one. A mature woman, who knows all the tricks of her trade."

"No." I turned my back on Saul, and like a nicotine addict desperate for a cigarette I plunged out of the stars' dressing room area to find my way past the Kravis's glass front doors to get fresh air outside.

Fool! I cursed myself for divulging my very personal info to Saul. I could imagine him hurrying to tell Fran about my ED problem. Then the two would get some belly laughs at my expense, and later join me, sneering.

Surprise! THAT didn't happen.

Instead I watched Saul and Fran berating each other as they managed the Kravis's giant twin stairway, modeled like the Paris Opera House's.

Beatrice Fairbanks Cayzer

Fran was fuming: "You're such an asshole. The pink dress suited me the best. That awful green number made me look like a snake."

"The pink was all ruffles and lace, for a teenage deb. You'd be laughed off stage in that. Now the green, with its sequins that could pass for fishscales, gave you the magic of a sensual mermaid."

"Saul, go fuck yourself! You, Rick, call for the car."

Fran dumped Saul, which was only a pale copy of Saul abandoning her to the flames at Beryl's house. I drove away quickly, without even a nod for a goodbye to Saul. I have ED, but I'm more of a man than that Saul, who left his lady love to an inferno while he escaped at top speed.

Goodbye, and GOOD RIDDANCE.

Fran's next order was very welcome. "I want us to return to England as soon as my Soviet Heiress has her run. That's Saturday, the day after my final performance in BOHEME. Get reservations."

Fine. Nothing could have suited me better. Miami had always been a bad luck place for me, what with receiving the news of Timmy's kidnapping at the Miami Horse Sales, and a year later being accused of murdering his father by the Blair teenager when we'd leased the house in a Coral Gables neighborhood.

Ouch, that reminded me of the second time I'd been unfaithful to my Happy. She'd been heavily pregnant with Irish, and I'd flown ahead to Miami where I'd met Lois Blair at the Seminole Indian Reservation's Casino. What a mistake that affair had been from beginning to its fatal end! Now that I have ED, will Happy be tempted to be unfaithful to me?

Horrible thought. I was biting my lip at it, when I deposited Fran at her crumbling mansion's pretentious door. She said, "You needn't play the silent type with me, Rick. I know you aren't going to fuck me, so skip the silent act."

I tipped my forehead with two fingers in a fake salute, but really there was absolutely nothing I could say to Fran. I'd saved her life a mere eight hours ago, and didn't want to listen to a complaint that sex wasn't on offer.

My car needed gas. I pulled it up to a self-service pump and did the American thing of unhooking the gas hose and filling my tank, then went inside the gas station to produce my credit card. Suddenly I felt like vomiting. I rushed to the Men's Room and filled a toilet bowl with last night's supper. My late reaction to last night's fire? Or was this bout of vomiting provoked by the thought that Happy might become unfaithful when time passed and I couldn't defeat the ED problem?

Chapter 11

Soviet Heiress duly did her stuff. From a position in the rear of the Gulfstream track's field she swooped on the leaders in her Three Year Old's Fillies Race to take the honors.

No silver cup for Fran, nor a watch for me from the Execs, but the purse was far greater than any of those which Soviet Heiress had won previously.

Fran, without a man in her crosshairs, was ready to return to her husband and their castle. We flew with my family of wife and children via British Airways directly from Miami to Heathrow, where an eager Jeremy stood in the line of waiting family members to embrace his errant songbird. "Your baby has grown so much you'll hardly recognize him," he crowed, after giving her a long kiss. He'd brought his uncle's vintage Daimler for Fran. I had to find my old

Volvo in the long-term car park then bundle Happy and our "chillun" into it for our short drive to dear Epsom.

"You damn well better produce an early filly for me," were Fran's parting words.

I did.

But days after Fran was on the blower to inform me that I was to prepare the most forward of her other fillies for a quick trip to Nice because she was going to sing there for some disgustingly rich Russian oligarch at a special evening in the local opera house.

Moreover on her return from Palm Beach she'd found a contract offering a huge sum for her to sing in Nice, in Ekaterina Semenchuk's favorite role in a concert version of BORIS GODUNOV, and expected me to run a filly at the nearby Cagnes Sur Mer racecourse.

My first duty at Epsom was to rush down the manure-strewn path to our stables to check on our horses. Most had their winter coats, which I loved to see. In winter as a boy I'd compared my Dad's hunters to my beloved teddybear. They had long heads and oval hooves, but in my imagination I could think of them as over-sized teddys. Paddingtom bear wearing racing colors on his blanket.

I checked out Fran's fillies. One or two had lost their wooly coats at the approach of March. With spring not far in the offing, I found one filly very advanced, both in appearance and at the gallops. Yes, I could safely ship her to Cagnes Sur Mer and expect her to win because English horseflesh did well there.

Happy, ever a good sport, didn't complain about packing up again for a move to Nice. "Ah's ready to go back where it's sunny," she said, with a kiss to follow. "Tough on ourn Timmy, to take him out o' school ag'in. But the warm weather will do Dorothy some good. She's startin' in with them sniffles."

No worry about little Richard. He's as pleased to travel as an astronaut. Timmy, as always, made a fuss. Not about leaving school, but because he'd hoped to join a team of forward rugger players. His intended sport. Horseracing was never what he wanted. Tim resented the love I gave our horses.

Nice is one of my preferred French cities. Its newly renovated international airport is clean and welcoming. I always find it remarkable that immediately upon exiting it you are right on the Eastern end of the Boulevard des Anglais, driving along a brilliant beach bordered by a midsection of palms and flowers in the center of the road.

Being Fran's guests, we were lodged in a back street hotel, on the level of a Bed & Breakfast. Called the Ombre, I could guess that it was a six-a-huit hotel that catered to illicit affairs. Too bad that the inviting kingsize bed in our room would get no action from me!

I would have preferred to be housed right in the middle of Cagnes sur Mer to save on transportation to the smaller resort. But no, Fran wanted me at her beck and call. Her hotel was the Westminster, a first class place on the seafront but not as expensive as the more renowned Negresco.

Fran, who had spent merely one night at the castle with Jeremy, had found a new boyfriend by the time I'd checked into the Ombre. His name? Frothington Howard. A dealer in very valuable sporting art, he'd zeroed in on Fran because he'd Googled her name and learned she owned racehorses. He was staying at the Ombre, which is why Fran had heard of this back street place. I took one look at his eagle-shaped head with its beak nose and predatory eyes, and I reckoned he'd have more success selling paintings to Fran than the real estate agents had with houses they'd tried to push on her in Miami and Milan. The only thing I liked about Fran's newest lover was his nickname: Froth. It suited him perfectly.

What I didn't like was the noise of his bed rocking over our heads when he made love to Fran.

In this cheap building the floors were junk, and his bed must have been positioned exactly over ours because he was in 506 while we were in 406. Tough on me, to hear lovemaking when I can't have any now.

The paintings he offered were not junk. He must have had them on consignment, because their combined value ran into the millions. If he owned any of those pictures he wouldn't have been rooming at the Ombre.

Among the painters in his catalogue of great sporting art, I counted the early masters Munnings, Degas, Sartorius, Herring, Alken, and a modern great: LeRoy Nieman.

I would have been more than pleased to own any one of them. Our disastrous financial situation certainly precluded any such joy.

With a week to spend touring until the first race at Cagnes Sur Mer, I asked Happy if she'd like to return to Monaco, a principality which had given us both such wonderfully ecstatic sex in years gone by.

"Sho 'nuf, Ah's got real won-der-ful memories of thet there place."

We rented the cheapest Renault at the nearby car agency, and took the Lower Corniche east to be able to enjoy the scenic route with its cascading villages, where each of those offered a different style casino building and quaint restaurants. We didn't stop to eat at any of them, although Timmy kept droning he wanted to go eat, at McDonald's, his favorite eatery.

Monaco had changed. In many ways for the better. Where before we'd had to watch carefully where we tread to avoid dog poop, the streets were now crystal clean due to poop bag machines on every corner. The over-abundance of extremely elderly invalids being pushed in wheel chairs by carers had lessened. I saw only one centenarian, and he hopped along on one leg thanks to an elbow-style crutch. A blesse' de guerre from God-knows-which battle—Dien Bien Phu? The Congo's, or Rwanda's?—this spritely oldster wore a bright and happy smile. Takes all kinds!

Our favorite restaurant had gone out of business. Probably because rents were higher and its menu held to low prices. A car agency stood in its corner site. We decided to please Timothy, and went to find Carrefour's building because McDonald's had a welcoming sign on the street next to the supermarket. Happy was pleased, having learned at various McDonald's around the globe that they provided free Internet service and she could text her Kentucky hills Pa. He was a cyber age junkie, with a Facebook, Tweeter, and www.page account to keep tabs on his daughter.

We averted our eyes when we drove past the endearing hotel on Monaco's dockside. It had such poignant memories of sublime sex. I recalled with passion how I'd responded to the siren call of waves crashing on rocks below the Hotel de Paris Spa. That superb sound had awakened additional sex delights I'd rarely experienced before.

Our tiny Renault climbed the high Monte Carlo hill to the old Opera House, which took up a corner of Garnier's mid-Nineteenth Century casino. I recalled with fervor how in years past I'd seen how handsome Prince Albert looked in the Royal Box, standing next to his father Prince Rainier.

Happy had commented: "Sad when y'all thinks how many times thet lovely Princess Grace sat there in thet Royal Box. Ah'd loved huh when she were a movie star in thet Dial M For Murder. She were so be-auti-ful! Smart too, Ah bet." While we passed its private entrance, a stately antique Rolls stopped at the open gate to bring the now reigning Prince Albert II to a performance. He'd matured, and wore a thoughtful expression that told me he was an Atlas with too many cares on his shoulders.

CARES were paramount when we found a parking space in front of the Café de Paris. We'd stopped to buy ice cream cones for the "chillun" from the open booth next door to the mini-casino haven for slot machine-addicts. Our Dorothy, who so seldom demanded anything, had pleaded for a chocolate cone. Happy had hesitated to comply, fearing that Dorothy's new dress would be heavily splashed with melted chocolate ice cream. But as I so often acceded to Timmy's demands, it was now my favorite's chance to get what she wanted. Little Richard was too low on either of our totem poles to make a request.

The CARES began when we sat down at a café table and were immediately joined by Merrily Gold. "Thank goodness, you two are in Monaco. I need help. I'm in mortal danger. Yes, of being killed here. Happy, help me. I've learned from Google how you solved eight murders. STOP this one from happening."

"Nine murders," Happy said pointedly. "Nine. Now, wut makes y'all think thet y'all's on a hit list? 'N wut y'all doin' here anyways?"

"I know my competitors want to murder me. I've seen signs. I'm in Monaco for a convention of leading cosmetic and perfume manufacturers. Surounded by would-be killers."

'This'here place be known fo' its safety reputation."

"Sure! Until it has another murder. Like when I get killed."

"'Nother murder?"

"Yes. Don't you read newspapers? There was that multi-millionaire who got suffocated in his 'ultra-safe' apartment just down this street. It was supposed to be an accident, that he barricaded himself and his nurse in a bathroom, when a fire was lit in his room. Suffocated. No accident! Not when you're a multi-millionaire."

Happy frowned. She's an avid reader of newspapers and resented the insinuation she never read one. "Sho, Ah's known about thet. Some years ago, weren't it? And the dead man's male nurse went to prison fo' settin' the fire. Yeah, 'n Ah knows about another murder, when a British couple were found weeks after their bodies began to stink in the Sun Tower. He were a real es-tate agent, 'n mebbe sufferin' from depression, shot his girl-friend 'n killed himself. But y'all has no reason fo' to be killed."

Merrily had grabbed the remainder of Dorothy's ice cream cone and was licking it. Between licks, she gasped, "I'm the queen of American cosmetics! Don't you realize how many of those newcomer princesses would like to be queen?"

"'N murder y'all? Ah ain't met any o' yourn com-pe-ti-tors, exceptin' thet po' darlin' Beryl Blum wut died in huh house fire in Palm Beach. Real, sweet gal. If's she were like wut y'all's talkin' about, Ah doubts there be many a killer in thet business."

"You'll meet a few here. There must be nearly a dozen want-to-bes. Every hotel that belongs to the Bains de Mer company, got full up last night with owners of cosmetic and perfume companies. The Hotel de Paris, the Hermitage, Hotel de Bay, and Old

Beach are all bursting at the seams. See that jitney bus unloading across the plaza at the Hotel de Paris? All cosmetic people staying at smaller hotels. In one of them is the would-be murderer. Happy, dear! You must help me."

My Happy, ALWAYS SO WILLING TO BE OF SERVICE, NOW HESITATED. I SUPPOSED SHE DIDN'T LIKE BEING PRESSURED.

In the silence, I caught Merrily eyeing Timmy's strawberry ice cream cone. Not for long! Timmy isn't easily parted from the food he likes. He gave her a look that would have done credit to Napoleon Bonaparte scolding a losing general.

Merrily filled the increasingly embarrassing silence: "I'd like strawberry ice cream, too. In a dish. Oh, and with chocolate sauce."

I nodded, and turned back to the ice cream stand.

"Non, Monsieur. We do not have any chocolate sauce," said the attendant, to my query.

Thinking of the fine, promising colt I'd bought for Merrily, that would be winning races this year, and well aware how she could pull him out of my stable at any time, I suggested: "Give two scoops. Strawberry on the bottom, chocolate on top."

Carrying the ice cream, in a fancy dish that told me it would be expensive, I returned to our table.

Happy was carefully replying to Merrily's demand. My Happy was also well aware that Merrily could take away her colt at will. Happy gargled: "Well Miz Merrily, as how y'all feel the need fo' help, Ah'd honestly suggest hirin' a body-guard."

"Done that. Got three. Eight hours duty for each. No Sundays or holidays off."

With a sigh, Happy gently cleaned chocolate from Dorothy's mouth and dress. She cleaned Baby Richard and changed his bib. With Merrily staring at her, expectantly waiting for more advice, Happy added, "Ah'd stay me close to Monaco. Not go up in no hills."

A shadow blocked out Monaco's late afternoon sun. A youngish woman stood facing Merrily. She said, "You're Merrily Gold, I believe. We had adjoining seats at the welcome party yesterday. I'm Ruthie Hall. I make the Ruthie facial products. Can I sit down?" She didn't wait for an answer, taking the empty seat next to Timmy.

Oh. Oh. Timmy isn't the easiest table partner.

Timmy licked his ice cream cone in double quick time. No way was he going to share it with this newcomer.

Ruthie Hall smiled. "Any chance for an ice cream for me? I like the soft kind." She giggled. Was that a double entendre indicating that she KNEW about my ED? Good God! Can Happy be a tattle-tale?

"Sure. Strawberry, or chocolate? Vanilla, maybe?"

"Make it a mixture of all three. A cassata."

Expensive. I began to wish we hadn't stopped at this café. A waiter hovered over our table like a vulture. He KNEW I was going to have a difficult time paying the bill. I wished he'd go away. I was doing the donkey work, carrying the ice creams. I hoped I wouldn't have to shove out a tip. The girl at the counter grinned mischievously. "Would Monsieur like a sabayon sauce with that?"

No! I pointed to the smaller scooper-outer. "Give me three petits."

It wasn't that I resented Ruthie Hall for intruding. I liked the look of the woman. She had broad shoulders almost good enough to run for the fifty yard line. Her eyes were honest, with a piercing know-it-all intelligence that neither dismayed me nor put me off.

The makeup she wore, which I assumed was her own line, had a discreet elegant look.

Happy warmed to her immediately. She asked the vulture waiter for two extra spoons, dug hers into the strawberry scoop on Ruthie's plate and handed me the other spoon to test the chocolate. Evidently we were going to be close friends with Ruthie.

Chapter 12

"Where y'all stayin'?" she asked Ruthie.

"The Hermitage. Love it. Great murals on the ceilings and turn-of-the-last-century art everywhere. Good view of the harbor."

"No ifs and buts?" I asked.

"Not really. Only what you can expect when you live above the port and a main artery road that connects Italy and France. Lots of traffic noise. Boats, and cars. I like hearing the boats calling passengers to hurry back before sailing time. Like that a lot."

"Very peaceful, these days. Although it wasn't always so. Did you know that during World War II right here in Monaco the Old Beach Hotel was the scene of a mini-massacre? I guess you could call it that, when Nazi officers and their wives or fancy women got mowed down when two British war planes strafed the Old Beaach's terrace after their pilots caught sight of the Nazi uniforms. Maybe flying back to a Malta air base from the battles in Greece. The Nazi officers and gals were sitting on the terrace eating ice cream, when raat-a-taat-taat they were sprayed by bullets from the planes. Honest! But nowadays Monaco's dropped in on by nothing more menacing than these humongous cruise boats we see below us at the new dock."

"Y'all from the mid-West? Not used to them big cruise boats?"

"How'd you guess? Indiana, that's my home state."

"Y'all has a real purty way of pushin' on them Rs. Now Miz Merrily here, she don't keep to huh home ac-cent. She be borned in Al-a-ba-ma. Not thet y'all could guess. She done tole me as she took el-o-cu-tion lessons in New Yawk. Lost huh purty ac-cent. Ah done took me el-o-cu-tion lessons in London. Ain't done me no good. Didn't stay with 'em."

Merrily bit out: "Because your business success didn't depend on speaking correctly. You say you talk to your horses. I don't think horses take exception to a Kentucky hills accent." Merrily's mouth hardly moved as she spat the words. She wasn't best pleased that Ruthie had joined our group. She took out her displeasure on my Happy.

We concentrated on the ice cream. I ate most of Ruthie's strawberry scoop. She left the chocolate for Happy. When all the ice cream had been devoured, and I was dearly hoping that Merrily wouldn't begin on the drinks menu, she stood up and left the table. She called from the steps of the Garnier casino: "Rick, keep me informed about my horse."

Ruthie asked politely: "You train horses?"

"Yes. Merrily's one of my owners. Bought a fine, promising colt for her."

"What's his name?"

"WOW!Me."

Ruthie giggled. Her perceptive eyes were laughing. "That sounds like Merrily wanted to plug her products' brand. Never misses a trick!"

Not too entranced that this young woman had come so swiftly to that conclusion, I said grimly: "No. She doesn't! I was surprised that Wetherby's would accept the name. It was such an obvious ploy to get free publicity."

Happy calmed the turbulence. "Miz Merrily, she done come a long ways from huh shack in Al-a-bama. Havin' to compete with all them famous companies: Chanel, Estee Lauder, Helena Rubinstein. Many, many others. Ah used huh products, until Ah learned me she adds cocaine in some t'git customers hooked."

"Don't believe that gossip. The Pure Foods And Drugs people wouldn't let her get away with something like cocaine in lipstick. I think she makes a damned good product. And I like her perfume for young girls. It was clever to aim at that market. I give credit where credit's due." Ruth scraped at her plate for the last vestige of vanilla ice cream.

I didn't order another plate of the stuff. It wasn't only that I worried about the size of my bill. I felt concerned that it could get back to Merrily that Happy had been chatting up a woman so obviously unpopular with her.

Could Merrily suspect this young person to be a potential killer? An upwardly mobile cosmetics "princess" who would be capable of killing the 'queen?'"

Ruthie didn't abandon the Merrily story. "I did hear she'd had a damned hard climb up the ladder. Probably used any number of tricks. Relied on industrial espionage."

"Wut be 'in-dust-rial es-pi-onage?'"

"Spying on competitors' new products. Mostly to incorporate the competitors' new ideas into your own products."

"Ain't rightly fair, be it? Ah doesn't know ifn Merrily need do thet. She seems to have plenty idees o' her own-like."

"What do you really know about Merrily?"

"Wut Ah seen on Google. "N wut she done told usn huhself."

"Did she mention her Egyptian husband? And her autistic son? Nothing's ever written or televised about either of them. Her publicity and advertising people make sure of that. Write them up or try to get the story on TV and NO MORE ADS from the WOW!Me company."

"She married an Eg-yp-tian? We'all went to Cairo last year. Were in the house of an Eg-ypt-ian when he were murdered. But Ah don't dwell on none of thet. Ah likes to recall seein' them pyra-mids, 'n goin' to Memphis, 'n up the Nile to Karnak. Mah poor son Timmy, he done got Nile tummy though. We'uns left Egypt to take him back to England."

"Nile tummy. He seems to have got over THAT very well. Isn't he on his second ice cream cone? But speaking of Merrily's worst problem, her son's condition has deteriorated. As a little fellow he ran and played almost like any other kid. Now he's got aggressive. Too much to handle. Or so she claims, which is why she stuck him in an institution. Big secret. But I know about it."

"How come? Y'all knows, when there ain't never nothin' on TV or in the noospapers!"

"A friend of mine has a little daughter in the same institution. She's poor. Struggles to pay her own rent, without the added worry of doctors or therapists for her child. It's a free institution. She learned about it on the internet. British Government pays the bills there. All you need is a British connection, fly to England, and deposit the kid."

"Merrily's got her a British conn-ec-tion?" Happy gasped, riveted, because she has a Brits husband too.

"The ex-Egyptian husband. Born in Alexandria, but has a British passport. Yeah, so the son's British. He's about thirteen, now. Bad age. Lost his childhood beauty. Was gorgeous as a kid. No longer. Has acne all over his face. Beats up the other kids if there's any lack of supervision. Kicks them. Bites them. Can't communicate, except by misbehaving. Yells a lot of gibberish. Same gibberish. Repeated over and over. My friend keeps her daughter at a distance, and is working on getting her transferred to another place."

I said, "How sad. Sad for Merrily. Sad for the son." I was walloped in my heart thinking of my own Timmy, and how for two years after his kidnapping experience Timmy wouldn't smile, or show affection towards anybody. Including Happy, and me.

Thank God for little Richard's birth, which jolted Tim back into normality.

Timmy was never out of my thoughts for long. Popping into his mouth the last crumb of his cone, he said, "Let's go back to McDonald's. I like a hamburger with my ice cream."

"Nah." Happy signaled I should pay the bill, but she wasn't about to accede to Timmy's usual demand. Shaking her curls, she said, "As Ah recalls, there be them Jardins Exotiques up high on the Monaco border. We should go see them. Great fo' Dorothy. She likes gardens. She—"

Ruthie interrupted. "I never feel it's very safe, leaving Monaco. Those roads up into the hills are havens for road pirates. They lurk watching out for tourists, attack them for their money, credit cards and jewelry. You want to stay down here near the port. Safer. Stick to the coast road if you want to go to Italy and see Veintimiglia or San Remo."

"Thankee fo' the ad-vice. But Ah guess as how anyways it were best to return to our ho-tel. Little Richard needs a change o' clothes. Wet right through. 'N mebbe Dorothy's too tired t'enjoy gardens to-day."

Our little party split up. I wondered if we'd see Ruthie again.

Chapter 13

We did. In a coffin.

Ruthie hadn't heeded her own advice. With our morning newspaper we got the story. She'd hired a limousine to drive her to Cagnes sur Mer, planning to watch the races. Her limo driver chose the Grande Corniche, high in the Alpes Maritimes.

Approaching the highway's toll booth a bomb had been detonated. Two cars in front of the limo were demolished along with Ruthie's limo. All passengers and chauffeurs were killed.

There wasn't much left of Ruthie to view at the Nice Mortuary. Her head and shoulders were still intact. We couldn't know how much of her remained under the covers that hid her trunk and legs.

We remained in Nice for the rest of the day.

Merrily had shown up at the Mortuary. She wanted company. And pressed us to join her for lunch. She led us to a local restaurant in the Court Selaya that had joined with others to take over the old Flower Market in the ancient part of the city.

Dominating the entrance to this area was a huge trompe-l'oeil mural depicting a man on a ladder painting a picture of a palm tree. The restaurant Merrily chose was called SAFARI. It specialized in the local delicacy called Socca. That's a concoction that looks like a pizza but has no cheese. It's made with chickpea flower and olive oil baked in a wood-stoked oven. Delicious. I think I could become addicted to it.

Merrily was lamenting having told Ruthie to use her limo service. "I've had the same chauffeur for at least three years, and now the poor man's dead. Blown up by that roadside bomb. His limo left a crater eight feet deep. I told you I'd need protection! Look at what's happened to Ruthie: our industry's dangerous. So many ambitious competitors. I think they'd stop at nothing to get their products to the top. Even kill!"

"Sho seem mighty ugly, this here business." Happy finished her pastry, and asked the waitress if she knew where the nearest McDonald's was located. Happy well knew that our Timmy wasn't going to be satisfied with his Socca.

I paid the bill, which was modest. I wasn't to get off so lightly. Merrily swung her waist-long mane like a filly, and suggested:

"Let's us go to the Negresco. I really prefer a first class place to slumming."

We strolled through the fresh produce market and a row of specialty shops offering local trinkets. Dorothy hung back lpoking longingly at the doll trinkets, her face pressed against the boutique's glass. My Dorothy looked like a beggar-child eyeing cakes.

I hailed a taxi. It was too far to be able to walk to the Negresco. Our driver took me for a casual tourist and tried to leave the Boulevard des Anglais to double the fare by entering crooked side streets, the streets' designed to repel cannon balls by zigzagging.

The old Negresco had the same towers I remembered as a boy, otherwise it was much changed. In the huge main lobby a bazaar of shops had back to back boutiques. These shops offered goods way beyond my meager pockets. Thank goodness, Happy didn't imitate Dorothy and glue her face to the windows. I couldn't have afforded a handkerchief! But Merrily, as a new owner, had to be cosseted.

In her considerate way, Happy chose to enter the luxury world's version of a coffee shop. Thank God, Merrily didn't complain and voice a preference for the bar where she could order champagne. The day had already cost me far more than what I'd budgeted.

And then, worse luck, Fran Cabrach showed up.

Of course pennypinching Fran had also chosen this coffee shop in preference to the champagne bar. She sat at a circular table, alone. On the table were propped several sheets of the Boris Gudonov music. She was mouthing the words to her main aria.

"Fran, honey!" Happy rushed to her table and kissed her on both cheeks, European style. My, how sophisticated my little jockey had become since she'd left her Kentucky hills! "Wut y'all doin' in this here ho-tel?"

"Oh, hello, Hap. Can't you see? I'm working on my role in tomorrow's opera. Do I need to remind you that I'm in Nice to sing? It's not all racehorses in my life."

Fran ignored Merrily. She hadn't warmed to Merrily since the Palm Beach fire. Very pointedly, she said: "I've put aside two tickets for you and Rick."

No offer of a ticket for Merrily.

"Is y'all expectin' a big crowd? 'N fancy-like? Do Ah need to purty-up?"

"What you're wearing will do." Fran gave Happy a head-to-toe look-over, partially sneering, partially envious of Happy's curvaceous body.

Fran dismissed us by opening her capacious handbag and removing eyeglasses, an affectation recently added to her list of HOW TO GET RID OF PEOPLE.

I chose a table at the far end, where an inviting coffee percolator was hospitably sending out a welcoming smell. After a nod from Merrily, I ordered three coffees. Happy looked over the menu and decided to make the children wait for McDonald's. I wanted to talk about Merrily's horse, but being cautious of Fran's intrepid hearing, I decided against any mention of possible races in case the one owner's expectations clashed with the other's.

We ended this long day at McDonald's.

I'd off-loaded Merrily at her rented penthouse. With the cosmetics industry convention having ended its time in Monte Carlo, she'd moved to a very new complex that offered tennis courts, a heated swimming pool and a splendid view of the Mediterranean.

What a relief to be able to enjoy my wife and children without the stress I always felt when in the company of any of my owners.

Chapter 14

The following evening, thanks to our hotel, we found a kindly thirtiesh woman to babysit our "chillun,' while we went to hear Fran sing. After the tragedy of losing our darling little Irish after she caught meningitis in Madrid from her teenage babysitter, I'd opted for mature women.

Cagnes Sur Mer's little modest hotel had also provided a light supper, perfect to fill our tummies before we left for the Nice Opera house to hear Fran emote in BORIS GODONOV.

I've always enjoyed the thrilling drive from Cagnes Sur Mer along the Boulevard des Anglais to reach the oldest part of Nice, where its exquisitely-designed Opera House had pride of place.

Its architecture was not as dramatic as the one Garnier gave to Monte Carlo. The heroic-sized human figures were missing for this city-placed music emporium. It had one identical feature: the yard wide doll house-like miniature theater with its rows of seats filled with tiny cardboard people forming a full-house audience.

Happy pressed the button that illuminated the toy theatre. "Lookee, it done got a chan-de-lier just like the one in thet movie "Phantom Of The Opera.""

It did. And we got a close look at the real chandelier because pennypinching Fran had given us seats high up in the top gallery. Great view. But a bit smelly, because most of the other members of this roosters'-gallery audience was made up of dirt-poor music students who had to choose between a bar of soap or a glass of wine. From the body odors it was apparent that many had opted for the wine.

Fran was in great voice. But hearing the music didn't fill me with ecstasy. I missed the gorgeous Russian costumes and décor that would have been part of a traditional opera when BORIS GODONOV is produced. This night there were no costumes, a blank background. Only the perfection of Fran's contralto and the deep, deep bass voice of the mentally-tortured Czar appealed to me. I detested the Director's idea of placing the star performers on high stools with corresponding music stands hiding the stars' faces.

Usually a five-hour performance, the Director had eliminated all of the chorus. There were only eight vocalists, the minor roles whittled out. There were still three hours of arias and duets.

At the end of the last act we wound down the five flights of unending stairs to be surprised by the sight of Merrily in the lobby.

"Meet my Number One Assistant, Jasmine," she enunciated each word with the perfection demanded by her elocution teachers. Merrily looked in top form.

In the street's dim light she could actually smile without fear of her wrinkles showing.

Happy was busily studying Jasmine's face. She'd seen plenty of Merrily's executives in these past weeks. This girl was special. Jasmine could have been the inspiration for the French description of a plain but attractive girl: Une Jolie Laide. Her hair had been cut by London's top professionals, dyed to a less than platinum blonde, and let to hang loose as if she'd just got out of bed.

She had three dimples, one in each cheek and one in her chin: deep dimples. When she laughed, which she did constantly as if laughing at some private jokes, Jasmine's presence lightened the Go-Home atmosphere that had pervaded the flood of opera buffs who were rushing to their cars or to the downtown bus station. They looked deflated, maybe these sophisticated buffs also didn't care for opera with no costumes, no décor, and the stars propped on stools.

Jasmine chuckled: "I've heard wonderful stories about the two of you from Merrily. Excuse me, I mean Mrs. Gold. How Rick fell off a horse trying to reach a dandelion for your little girl Dorothy. And Happy—may I call you Happy, Mrs. Harrow—when you opened up a crate your father sent from Kentucky, expecting his rooster-comb cure for suffering horses and the crate had nothing but moonshine illegal liquor!" She roared.

A splendidly antiquated Rolls Royce drew up to us at the curb. No tacky stretch-limo for Merrily in the South of France! She'd learned what impresses and made what she'd learned her Ten Commandments. Stretch limos a no-no. Antiques, yes. She carried off a clever maneuver getting to the car's regal back seat. Melody pushed Jasmine in first so that it was her bikini underpants that flashed to spectators on the street. Jasmine never dropped a giggle any more than if she'd been knitting she'd drop a stitch.

Skimping on her words, Merrily clucked: "I could give you two a lift. If your car isn't too far away. Won't catch me crossing the Var."

Always the diplomat, Happy purred like a cat who knew who'd give her milk. "Ah thinks as we'd just as soon walk, thankee."

I wanted a lift. As so often happened lately, my feet were giving trouble. Aching.

I leaned into Merrily's antique Daimler and gently pushed Happy's rear on to a jump seat while I grabbed the other seat. I didn't understand why Happy hadn't accepted Merrily's offer. In my book of How To Treat Owners rule number thirteen had to be accept gratefully whatever an owner offers even if it's a turd.

Delighted that we were included, Jasmine prattled enthusiastically about Fran's make-up. "That one won't need a face-lift. Hardly any powder or blush-on. She's got great high cheekbones, and that wonderful powder-puff mouth."

Merrily said "Too bad she's hooked up with that dealer in fakes, Frothington."

I kept my mouth firmly shut. No good spilling the beans about Fran's miserliness, profligacy, and double standards. First, I had to remain faithful to my main owner. Secondly, I recognized that here with Jasmine I could be in the presence of a genuinely good woman who would never use negative descriptions to flagellate a woman of real talent.

None of us caught a glimpse of Fran's exit from the theater. Because she hadn't worn a costume and no stage make-up, our Fran had decided to mix with her fast departing audience. No one recognized her, which must have been a hiccup for Fran's sense of self-importance.

Happy seemed disappointed not to have had an opportunity to give an "Hi-ya, y'all" to Fran.

Into a void created by silence, Jasmine bleated, "Myself, I never wear much make-up. Or perfume. Strange when you consider my first name, and that I work for a company that sells BEAUTY PRODUCTS. But I'm a contented bunny. Life's good. Look around us at this magical city. Lights that glisten, lights that flicker. Ancient buildings. Newest discos. It's sheer enchantment. And we just heard the greatest two singers on the planet. Tomorrow, I'll be back at the job I adore, in London. My hometown. I can't ask for more."

Happy gave her moon-on-its-back smile. "Yeah, Ah feels thet-a-way often, too."

Jasmine continued to advance the conversation, like a horse that had broken its traces there was no stopping her: "I wish that darling Merrily here and Fran would be good friends. Fran has no control over what she says, or the loathsome language she uses.

But I wish that Merrily hadn't said that she thought Fran's Frothington sold fakes."

Merrily snapped, "Careful, Jasmine. You're going too far with that remark. All I said to Fran was to be careful. That all of Froth's treasures might need second opinions. It's Fran's fault that she didn't take that as kindly as I meant it."

Thank God we'd reached the car park where I'd left the rental Renault. I didn't want to be a witness to trouble between Jasmine and Merrily.

The car park wasn't locked. A very elderly man, old enough to have served in World War II, rattled keys and led us to our car. We'd waved goodbye to Merrily and Jasmine. I tipped the wobbling oldster, and Happy snuggled close to me as I buckled up her safety belt.

Neither of us tried any type of foreplay. Not on. Without a word ever spoken, we'd agreed to bypass my ED problem and enjoy the blissful love we shared. We'd had seven years of superlative sex, and that was over. We'd turned the page, and found very many other pleasures: the neighing of a sound horse. The giggles of joyous infants. The splash of a wave. Green awnings from fat trees. Moonbeams dancing in dust! The touch of a caring hand.

Happy was asleep by the time we reached our bed & breakfast type hotel in Cagnes-Sur-Mer.

Chapter 15

Its racecourse is shared by contrasting activities. There are flower shows, wine sales, and wedding parties. The big profits come from Les Trotteurs races, that are as popular in France today as they were once in the USA. These races feature a jockey seated in a light two-wheeled horse-drawn chariot. I call a sulky a chariot because I like to think that in ancient times Roman warriors went to battle in vehicles such as these. Otherwise the racing was similar. The jockeys vie to get to the finish line, and the fastest horse wins. Maybe.

I've never depended on making my living with such horses. The horses are wonderful, but there's so much shady stuff that happens in that world that I will remain steadfast to flat racing in my own country, or where its rules prevail.

There was one particular race that I'd had in mind for Fran's best filly, although actually I would have preferred to keep the filly from any racecourse. She's a great mover, persistent, and has guts. Moreover, she's really fast. I would have liked to keep her at home working and then show her off at Royal Ascot.

But that favorite event was still months ahead, and greedy Fran wanted her filly to earn whatever money was available so early in the Spring. Pennypinching Fran would never send a filly to Dubai, Australia, or South Africa, where great purses were for the taking. She'd settled for the south of France.

Happy had spent many hours at the Cagnes Sur Mer racecourse, familiarizing herself with the facilities and the going. On the afternoon of Fran's race, Happy looked as stressed as a mother cat that's misplaced one of her kittens. "Ah's not best pleased. Y'all knows as Ah talks to ourn string. Soviet Kitten tell me she ain't com-fort-able in the running he-ah."

She was shaking her curls while talking to me at the rails. A shadow fell over her face, blotting out the Mediterranean sunshine.

The blotting was produced by Froth, Fran's art gallery-owner newest boyfriend.

"Hello, you two. Seen Fran?" He was curt, not exactly rude, just to the point.

I said. "She's not here yet. But she'll show. Her race is about to come up."

"She won't be coming to the rails. Will she? Shouldn't we go find the filly? Surely, Fran will want to watch all the preparations made for this race."

Preparations? Two years of hard workouts on our stables' gallops. Taught to wait for the gate to rise, and then not lag behind the leaders at the start. Find the most favorable position. Get a second wind. No. Fran had not been present for all those preparations. "Soviet Kitten will do all right. I wouldn't run her otherwise. Happy will saddle her up."

Happy did. She was testing the buckle on the filly's belly strap when Fran arrived, breathless. "Soviet Kitten ready for this?" Fran's usual contralto voice had raised an octave.

"As ready as she'll ever be," I led this fine filly to the paddock. We waited patiently for her jockey. He arrived tardily, also breathless. Fortunately, when remembering the disaster in Spain when I couldn't communicate with our jockey because he didn't speak English and I don't know any Spanish except 'Gracias,' this boy not only spoke my language but he could ride like hell.

An Irishman, Mike Sullivan, he'd grown up in racing stables. He knew the game, and loved it.

Enjoying this milder climate in the South of France, Mike Sullivan immediately responded to the feel of a truly capable animal between his boots. Happy had given him a leg up, and Mike led out his mount with the assurance he could win the race.

He did. There was one moment when I feared he'd left it too long to make his challenge. But Mike knew his business and performed correctly Soviet Kitten matured into a grown-up once she'd savored the excitement of passing other fillies. I could see that Fran was going to have a lot of fun with Soviet Kitten.

Because her new boyfriend was present, Fran invited us for champagne.

We four went into the bar area, leaving our groom to deal with Soviet Kitten. There had been no prize other than the money for this race, so we were free to join our owner. Fran was not in the best of moods in spite of her filly's brilliant win.

"Damn all!" Fran had watered down her swearing around Froth. "Why on earth did we come to this tinny little racecourse? My filly could have won anywhere!"

Rule Number Fourteen for trainers. Never contradict an owner, even when she forgets she came up with the plan under discussion. I said nothing.

Froth wasn't so careful. Over his flute of champagne he made his sales pitch, mistakenly believing this was a good time to hit on Fran. "Why don't we make a date for an afternoon in London, between morning and evening stables, when the Harrows can join you—dearest Fran—to view three superb masterpieces so suitable for a winning owner like you."

Crafty Fran, who'd like to keep the boyfriend and her money, silkily muttered: "Work out a date with Rick. I know that either Wednesday or Thursday would suit me. No rehearsals for my next mega album."

I opened my 2011 datebook. "Thursday would suit. Merrily has invited Happy to a HUGE bash she's giving that day. But she didn't invite me, so I'm free to come to your gallery."

Froth smirked. "I've a Munnings, a Sartorious, and an Alken for you. The best of the Twentieth Century, best of Nineteenth, and best of Eighteenth."

With Fran nodding acceptance, I felt I could leave her in Froth's company and I gave Happy the look which in the past six years had always meant: "Let's get out of here."

The following week, promptly on the Thursday afternoon, having returned to England, I set out for London, leaving Happy trying to select what dress to wear to Merrily's party.

I drove from Epsom to London in record time, followed instructions how to drive into Bury Street having paid the Congestion Charge, and pulled up our Volvo to the street number Froth had given to me.

There was no gallery on the ground floor. A sign with his name, and a hand with its index finger pointing upwards, led me to sharp stairs that opened out to the First Floor. Fran and Froth were bickering over the painting of a fallen horse. I took a quick look and recognized Herring's palette. The horse belonged to a hunt. No racehorse, and not suitable for Fran.

"You made me climb those stairs for this?" she barked, pointing to the horse that appeared to have broken his back in his eagerness to join a hunt passing in the distance.

"This is an original Herring work. Read the signature: John Frederick Herring, Senior."

"Forget it. This is a hunter. I want a racehorse. And a racehorse that's fit. Not with a broken back."

Like a wily trainer, Froth didn't argue the point. He left us to poke around the innards of his so-called gallery and emerged with a fine oil of a healthy racehorse by Sir Arthur Munnings.

"Like it?" Froth's voice had become oily.

"How much? In pounds, not guineas."

"One hundred and ten thousand."

"But I could buy a decent filly for that much!"

"Darling Fran, you have fillies. But no Munnings."

"Forget flogging any painting to me for one hundred and ten thousand pounds." Fran's tone had flattened as it always did when she turned down an expensive colt I'd offered.

Froth scurried away. He was gone a considerable time. When he returned he had three more canvases with him. "An Alken, a Sartorious, and a Herring," he said.

He didn't have a chance to show them to Fran.

An enormous explosion broke the windows of his so-called gallery. We three rushed to the stairs, but could see nothing. Froth locked up his treasures. We three hurtled to the sidewalk. There were dozens of curiosity seekers milling around the street.

I asked a harried policeman, "What happened?"

Too busy to give a complete answer, in a surly tone the policeman replied: "Gas pipe explosion, farther down the road."

We could see flames and smoke coming from nearby. Worse, we began to breathe human ashes like from the chimney of a crematorium. I thought of New York's 9/11 disaster, when the two planes flew into the twin towers of its Trade Center, and how for days after there were human ashes floating in the air.

Walking briskly with the curiosity seekers, I reached the site of the explosion. We were on a crescent that had held a row of identical buildings, all painted white with black doors and pillared porticos. Like the gap in a mouth where a front tooth has been pulled, one building had left a hole full of flaming debris. Rubble. Parts of furniture. Lots of broken glass. Bits of scorched wallpaper. Twisted metal. We were soon pushed aside by rescuers from the local police station, A fire engine appeared, and its intestine-like hoses were uncoiled and began to pour water on the pile of debris that had been Number 42.

The houses on either side were numbered 41 and 43.

It was Number 42 that had vanished, "Oh, no. Please God, not Merrily's corporate building! That's where my Happy had headed to go to Merrily's party. Happy! My Happy!"

I prayed for a miracle.

A miracle duly happened. I heard Happy's Kentucky Hills accent. "Rick-honey. Thank God Ah's found y'all. I was afeered Ah'd miss a ride home if'n y'all weren't at thet gallery with Fran no mo'e." Happy, her face creased with anguish, was wearing the jeans and jersey she'd had on for morning stables.

I wanted to crush her into my arms. No way. She was carrying our little Richard, asleep in her arms.

"Our baby boy? Up in town? Why?"

"Ah's missed Merrily's par-ty. Soon's y'all left Ah's seen a nasty rash all over Richard's chest. Ah's rushed him to ourn doctor in Epsom. But he say Ah's got to take Richard to the Great Ormond Street Children's Hos-pi-tal in London."

"And the doctor found, what?"

"He say Richard all-er-gic. Probably to pea-nuts. Ah recalled thet Timmy gave him some o' hisn peanut butter sandwich. She 'nuf, thet doctor said the rash could be from thet. To ab-so-lutely never let him eat peanuts. He could die." Breathless from running down the opposiste street, Happy only now commented on the ruins of Number 42. "BUT RICK-HONEY, WUT-ALL BE THIS HERE MESS? THE WOW!Me BUILDIN' GONE, 'N ALL THE EMP-LOY-EES DEAD, WITH THEIR GUESTS!"

"Explosion. The place was blown up towards the end of the Wow!Me's company party."

Happy kissed Richard gently and handed him to me. "Let's usn go into thet café at the far end of this street. Ah wants to learn me mo'e o' wut caused the ex-plo-sion."

"You'd reached this street when it happened?"

"Sho 'nuf. Seen it, heard it. Horr-ible! Lucky Merrily weren't at the party. She called me this mornin' t'tell me not to expect to see her. Most folks at the party would be junior ex-ec-u-tives from other cos-met-ics and per-fume com-panies wut sent them to the con-fer-ence in Monaco. Them wut made friends with her ex-ec-u-tives there."

"Jasmine!"

"Nah. She'd be with Merrily."

We noticed that a young war veteran had entered the café. He was missing an arm, with his jacket sleeve pinned up to the empty elbow. He wore a prosthetic leg. Shaking, like a soldier who suffers from shellshock, he held out his good arm for balance and slid into a chair at the table next to ours.

I asked: "You all right? Anything we can do?"

He shook his head, and brought his trembling hand to his unshaven chin. "Haven't heard anything like that since Iraq, when I got mine. Same deal. Grenade."

"A grenade?"

"Sure. I heard the sound of the grenade's pin when it had been pulled out and hit the tiles of this café's doorway."

Happy, her eyes very alert, scoured the floor near us, found the grenade's pin, and slipped it into her purse. "Why-all a gre-nade be used fo' a gas ex-plo-sion?" she queried the veteran.

"Probably because Number 42's building was sound. Nothing wrong with its pipes. Any more than with all the other houses on this crescent. To blow it up, a grenade thrown at an exterior pipe would do the trick." The young veteran waved to the café's one waiter: "A brandy, please."

Happy looked as stricken as if she'd seen a hawk dive to kill a father grouse: the father grouse would have flown towards the hawk to lure it away from his hen and fledglings. "Ah thinks as Ah's goin' to throw up," she said, and lurched to the café's uni-sex toilet.

When she emerged, she found me sharing a brandy with the veteran. She said: "Ah thinks as we-uns be headin' home." She felt for Richard's nappy. "Richard be wet. Let's go."

I'd parked our Volvo in a nearby hotel's facility. Paid up, although I hadn't been an hour in the place, and pointed our car's hood to Epsom. We didn't talk, so as not to wake up Richard.

Chapter 16

The next day, after morning gallops, I found Happy, on our bum warmer, devouring the newspapers' version of the loss of WOW!Me Enterprises' London headquarters. Three newspapers printed lists of the names of outstanding young leaders of the cosmetics and perfumes industry who had died in the explosion.

Most of the papers went with the gas pipe story. Two called for tighter inspections of residential gas pipes, with a Labor MP berating the Conservatives for not having tightened them up before yesterday's tragedy. A repeat story about a San Francisco gas pipeline disaster of two years ago recalled that the Pacific Gas and Electric officials had acknowledged it briefly raised the pressure to the legal limit of 400 pounds per square inch for two hours before the fatal blast. It had leveled 38 homes and killed eight people.

Happy was wearing her 'Y'all don't fool me' expression when she gave a tearing yell.

"Rick-honey, there be a list of guests wut ac-cepted fo' thet party. Jasmine's name be on it!"

"I'll telephone the WOW!Me headquarters in New York for news of Jasmine."

"Yes, please. Thankee. Strange how none of these heah noospapers ain't sent no reporter to talk to them folks at the café. The Iraq veteran, fo' instance.'

I had Merrily's New York Office's number, and dialed it.

Engaged!

All the civilized world must have been dialing it at the same time.

Finally a bottled inhuman voice clicked into my ear:"WOW!Me Enterprises. We offer the best in the forefront of cosmetics, the most exquisite perfumes, and the tops in facecreams. Please leave your number and we will return your call. Have a good day."

Yuk. I tried Jasmine's home number printed on the card she'd given me when we'd first met. No reply.

Our telephone rang. Happy grabbed the receiver. "Merr-i-ly? Thet be y'all? Thank God fo' skippin' yourn party. Where-all be y'all?"

"In the North. Went to see my son. I know you know all about him! Jasmine, who is getting too big a mouth, must have told you. It's such a struggle to keep having him diagnosed. He's withdrawn. Body rigid, unless it's that he's flown into one of his tantrums. Ghastly. But as a mother it's my duty to go see him now and then."

"Merr-i-ly! Jasmine? She-all went up No'th too?"

A petulant sigh. "No. I imagine she went to the party at our London HQ. That would have been her duty."

"Ah, no!" Happy shouted in pain. "Wut y'all—"

"I've phoned you because I'll need a decent black suit for the funerals of those who were burned to death. I've heard the list. One of my American executives left the party early. He gave me the names. Yes, Jasmine's was among those gone missing."

"Merr-i-ly, Ah cain't think of no clothes. Ah's beat up over all them folks wut died. AND Jasmine."

"I know you're down in the country. But you can catch a train and go to Harvey Nick's. There's an underground station very near. Across the street, in fact. I'm still a size 10. I think a straight skirt would be best, and not too short. Not under the circumstances. A pretty suit. I'm sure there will be loads of paparrazi at the funerals. I want to look my best."

I took back the receiver. Happy was making a fist out of fury.

She shook her head violently while I told Merrily: "She'll pick out a suit. How much do you want to spend? Any favorite designer?"

"They tell me the 'in' person is Tomas Something-that-ends-in-ski. Oh, not more than two thousand pounds. And a hat. Black, of course." She rang off.

Happy's face had turned red with suppressed anger. She muttered: "Ah knows how bad we needs owners. But Ah thinks we'd best get us rid o' Merrily. Seems like she works under a cloud wut rains dead bodies."

"You're 100 per cent right about being desperate for new owners. In Merrily's case, I also CARE enormously for her colt. He's simply magnificent. I'm planning to send him to Newbury for an easy two-year-old season. Next year I'll aim him for the Wokingham at Royal Ascot, the Stewards' Cup at Goodwood, and, if he keeps in training, the Ayr Gold Cup. He could be named Sprinter Of The Year."

"Rick-honey," Happy's voice went to a gentle purr, "Why not ask ourn Saudi Prince to make Merr-i-ly 'an offer wut she cain't refuse?' Like we done when Hal took over thet there El Milagro?"

"Happy, she doesn't need any money. She's a millionairess. Maybe a billionairess."

My darling wife sighed. She left our bumwarmer to climb the stairs to change into London clothes. Minutes later she returned, dressed in an Ascot suit of two years previously, and a pashmina against the early-spring cold.

"Give me them keys fo' the Volvo," she said dully.

I was left home to babysit our "chillun."

She didn't come home until evening stables when she flew through our short front door. "Rick-honey, guess who-all Ah's seen? Bruno, ourn tenor friend from Milan! He be stayin' in the same buildin' in London as Merr-i-ly. Ah hopes he done found love ag'in today. Deserves to. After all thet tra-g-edy."

Bruno! I hadn't liked him at first. Could hardly stand his arrogance. His constant talk about his prowess in the sex department, and his boasting of huge amounts paid for opera parts hardly would have endeared me to him when I suffer now from ER and am in a constant state of near-bankruptcy.

My mind-set made a ninety degree change when on the night before his wedding to Happy's friend Nina, the bride-to-be was murdered and her body mutilated. We were together that night, which happened to be his premiere in the role of Cannio in Pagliacci. He made opera history with his rendition of VESTI LA GIUBBA. Earned him a million in royalties later when sold as part of an album. The tearing misery of learning his bride's fingers had been cut from her body was the catalyst for Bruno to give one of La Scala Opera House's audiences longest standing ovations.

We'd found him raging and weeping in his dressing room, having minutes previously been given the terrible news of Nina's murder. Happy and I had tried to comfort him, and to dissuade him from appearing on stage for the next act. Bruno sang anyway. We'd spirited him out of his dressing room later to avoid paparazzi, and the volcanic fury of Nina's mother who'd been trying to beat him with a stick.

Aside from pity, I was spurred to like Bruno when he commented: "I never hit woman. Nina's mother right to hate me." He'd left for his New York opera season immediately afterward, and we hadn't heard a word from him since.

Upstairs, while Happy divested herself of her tired Ascot finery, I asked: "Bruno, in Merrily's block of flats? And he's in love with Merrily?"

"Nah. Ah's goin' t'fill y'all in from the beginnin' when Ah's left Harvey Nichols with a black Tomas suit, and a matchin' stovepipe hat. Walked the walk to Merrily's. Was givin' her par-cels to the do'r-man when Merr-i-ly's limo pulls up to the sidewalk 'n she starts to unload her suitcases. Three, fo' an overnight stay! Gives hell to thet driver fo' not be willin' fo' to help. Then a scared-lookin' pale sort of furrin girl, probably in her Twenties, slides out o' thet limo. She takes over all three suitcases. One in each hand 'n the smaller one tucked under her right arm.

"Meet Basha, a new friend," Merr-i-ly thunders at me, 'n marches into yon lobby. Where, as strange as ifn hogs c'd fly, was Bruno. He been collectin' his mail. When he seen me he come rushin' to kiss me, but stopped like a deer caught in headlights, to stare at this-here Basha."

"I thought you said she was a pale, scared looking woman."

"Ah's fo'got to add she be a real-and-true be-auty?"

"Okay. My darling wife, you forgot that interesting fact. Go on. I'm fascinated." I sat down on our bed and relished my wife's beauty as she slowly undressed.

"Yeah, man. A be-auty. And nice, no sourpuss. Ah hates when anger ruins be-auty. Ah's figured her to be Swe-dish, o' mebbe No'wegian, But she stuck out her hand when the do'rman took them suit-cases, and in-tro-duced herself. She say to me:"I Basha Lewendolski. From Poland. My Eng-lish not too good. Mrs. Merrily say she give me ride to Lon-don. We met at hospital. My daughter Anya, she diagnosed autistic, and same age as son of Merrily."

"This is interesting me."

"Sho got me in-ter-ested. Ah done asked as what she do fo' a livin' but she ain't give me no answer."

"Will you ever see her again?"

"Don't rightly knows as Ah will. As Pa would say: Time will tell."

Chapter 17

Two days later Happy heard sharp raps on our five foot door. The door of our cottage was smaller than most because the people who built it in the Sixteenth Century must have been LITTLE.

I opened the door. Bruno stood there with an arm around a pale, frightened-looking beauty. Basha?

The woman was too tall for our doorway and stooped low to enter our lounge. Ouch. My father hated the word parlor, he preferred drawing room. Bruno filled the doorway, but as he was short, he didn't need to stoop much.

In his resonant tenor tones, he said: "Meet Basha. Your Happy tell my Nina she could live with you here. I bring Basha." Bruno's voice cracked, "As Nina no more alive."

What a quandary! Our cottage wasn't adequate for longtime visitors. Happy and I shared a room, as did our two boys. Amah slept with Dorothy. But for overnight guests we'd only a box room we'd fitted up for short stays if an owner happened to be caught here when a storm blew up that prohibited the use of our perpendicular driveway. "Uh, hello Bruno. How do you do, Basha. Wait, here. I'll go call my wife."

Happy, who'd heard the banging on our door, had changed out of a nightgown into jeans. Her curls weren't combed. I believe she'd drifted off to sleep.

"Bruno, y'all brought Basha to usn?" She couldn't say more. A huge yawn interrupted.

"You tell my Nina she could live with you. That, before she move into my apartment in Milan. She be alive now if she come to you. Please, offer hospitality."

"Sho nuf. Come over to the fire. What y'all want t'drink? Ate some supper? We got the leavin's from ourn po'k dinner. Get y'all two plates in no time." Happy took Basha's thin coat. Looking down at Basha's shoes, Happy noticed something she'd never seen even among her Kentucky Hill country 'po'r folks.' Basha's two shoes weren't a match.

"Yes, please. Dinner. Most kind." Basha drew herself to the fire. She hesitated to sit on our bumwarmer. I doubt she'd ever seen one in Poland. Ours was made of brass with a cushioned leather surround on the top, comfortable to wedge your backside close to the fire.

Bruno brought out a bottle of champagne from under his overcoat. He wore a very dramatic outfit. His coat had a fur collar; beaver, I imagine. His suit, cut in Romania some years ago, had narrow pinched shoulders and pleated trousers. Awful.

Without asking, he popped opened his champagne gift and the bottle poured its golden liquid on to the wide boards below. Of course the champagne was warm from the heat of his body. But, resourceful Bruno found my ice bucket with its regimental insignia, and he plunked the bottle square among the cubes.

Happy, with a lot of welcoming 'yes, you must stay' and "are you warm enough" supplied glasses for the four of us. She left Basha's side to go to the kitchen and carve slices off the pork bone we'd found too tough at supper. We'd left most of the thing.

She offered steak knives to Basha and Bruno in hopes they could carve some edible meat from the bone. Basha went at her portion with gusto. Bruno played with the ready slices and didn't bother to cut any more. His heavy frown indicated he'd much on his mind other than food. To be helpful, Happy said, "You two can have our kingsize bed."

"Mrs. Happy, you show me room for Basha. Not your bed. Guest room's. I sleep sofa."

He put down his plate and followed Happy up our vertical staircase that had been built in Shakespeare's time.

The room was shabby. Happy had found a coverlet at the church rummage sale. The curtains didn't match. My father's extra suits hung in the wardrobe, giving off an old man's odor. He left them in the converted spare room on the odd chance the weather would deteriorate during his visits from Warwickshire, and he'd have to stay with us beyond the time his small suitcase provided enough clothes. There was his toothbrush in a glass on the basin, and a shoehorn on the counter. The bed was narrow.

When he rejoined Basha and me, I heard a welcome comment. "Two people not fit in that bed," Bruno growled., referring to the guest room's single bed.

He seemed sad. He wasn't like the elated bridegroom-to-be I'd seen before Nina's tragedy. Why? For a man who'd boasted to me about his prowess in the romance stakes, hadn't he managed to get Basha into bed?

Had he forgotten his own advice? "Treat a woman like a skittish horse, use both hands and make sure they do magic."

Basha excused herself and went upstairs, where Happy was waiting to lend her a nightgown. Nightgown? I doubted Basha would need one.

Left alone with Bruno, I helped Bruno finish off his bottle of champagne. He became exceedingly glum. The champagne had the opposite effect from what was intended.

What was the matter?

Garrulous Bruno didn't hesitate to tell me. As he had in Milan in our Pensione's Men's Room, he proceeded to detail his sex life. "Terrible. I cannot do it."

I could certainly sympathize with that! Oh, oh, it sounds as if he is suffering the saddest illness of our century: LONELINESS.

He continued, worse than glumly: in an absolutely miserable tone, "I see my Nina above me in every bed. So sweet. Girl I love so much. Cannot, CANNOT replace my Nina."

"Understandable."

"There more. This Basha, beautiful. Da. But she tell me she have many, many men. For money. Too many. Man like me cannot accept. Maybe accept if she do that in past, if in past. She tell me it happening now. To pay for her child's rehabilitate."

"Uh, huh."

"Donc, I pay. Cannot do IT. Basha try help. No good."

"Bruno, why on earth did you bring her down here?"

"In Milan, your wife tell me story of sick child from Australia, she help. Child brought to sanctuary, your wife and its mother pray and child cured. Your Happy, she do special things."

"But, autism? I don't think she could really help . . ."

Bruno, sweating like a horse that had just recently been castrated, moaned: "Cost forty-eight thousand pounds a year in rehab place. Rehab? Those children never better get."

"Four thousand a month! So that's why Basha's been selling herself. And that's been going on for how long?"

"Since leave Poland. Never in Poland. She seamstress in Poland. Arrive Britain, sell sex for money to send kid to specialists. No job in Britain."

I began to think it was unwise of Happy to offer up our bed. What was gong to happen in it tonight?

There wasn't much time to speculate. Happy came downstairs with a huge grin making her freckles dance. She sang out, "Basha's in bed."

Like a virgin unwilling to sin, Bruno gave me one last comment. "Before, I never pay for sex. Girls, women all age, they offer go bed after hear me sing.

In Romania, in United States. Almost everywhere, except Bali. Muslims, in Bali."

With Bruno trudging unwillingly up our ancient stairs, I turned to Happy and drew her to where the dying embers still sent heat to our bumwarmer. "Bruno isn't making love to Basha. He can't. He says he sees Nina between him and any woman he tries to bed."

Happy nodded. "Not a ghost. Just the miseries. Wut could Ah do t'help?"

"Forget it. When Bruno falls in love, he falls hard. We know. We saw how he dumped rich and famous Fran, the bona fide Countess, for Nina. A girl who had no money of her own, dependant on her mother's new husband. Now I think he's fallen for Basha. God knows Bruno could afford to support her and pay for the daughter's keep in that place for autistic children. But he's disgusted by her profession, and it hurts his pride to pay for lovemaking."

"Mebbe thet little daughter ain't got the aut-ism. Ah's read in noospapers thet the autism misery be dif-fi-cult to di-a-g-nose."

"Wishful thinking, my darling. If she's in an autism place, good doctors sent her there because she has autism."

"Don't y'all believe thet. Doctors can be wrong. Often they be too busy t'take much notice."

"Happy dear, just because those two are under our roof doesn't mean you've got to take on all their problems."

"Ah's not meddlin' none." Happy gave me a kiss. Not a foreplay kiss. A peck on the cheek. Ever since my ED problem she didn't believe in either of us getting too excited when there wouldn't be a thrilling end to the foreplay. Or any end. Sighing, she said: "Ah's just got me some thinkin' to do."

She collected the used glasses, tossed the empty champagne bottle in the bin, and collected a blanket for me from under the stairs.

The blanket was a silent request for me to sleep on our sitting room's sofa. That night Bruno felt cured from his 'can't do it.'

Chapter 18

Happy did her thinking for most of that night. She'd discovered that the guest bedroom was cold and its bed was damp. In the morning she put on her jeans, and a sweater covered by her windbreaker, selected two pairs of socks one on top of the other, and met me at our front door to join me for morning stables.

A cruel wind was blowing. There was sugar-like snow on the new Spring grass. A cuckoo scolded from our nearby woods as we trudged down our driveway.

Ice covered the manure there, keeping our boots pristine.

"Sleep well?" I asked.

"Nah. But Ah's got me a idée fo' helpin' Basha some. We's goin' t'invite her to bring thet chile o' hern here. Ah needs t'study thet chile."

"Where would she sleep? We've got a full house."

"Don't give thet no mind. Ah's seen them blow-up mattresses at Target. Y'all get me one and Ah's usin' ourn bicycle pump to get it full up of air. Put it in the pantry next to the kitchen, where ourn Aga can keep her warm."

"Happy darling, I'll gladly buy the mattress. But what makes you think the girl can be helped? She may not even speak English."

"Some folks says as Ah don't speak English! Kentucky-talk, thet's wut Ah speaks, 'no shame admittin' to it." Happy giggled. "Tell y'all somethin', Rick-honey. Ah re-calls as how ourn friend Maheen told me she re-acted bad as a kid when she-all learned-her thet her mother slept with men fo' money. Real-negative like. Plenty tantrums. Mebbe thet's wut ails this chile. Ain't no autism. Ah plans me to show thet chile how animals mate. Chickens too. Ah's read somewhere thet the Dalai Lama were asked how could he counsel folks on marriage when he ain't never been married? He done answered thet he watched birds, how they mated. Ah's got plenty chickens in ourn yard, 'n a really over-sexed rooster. Ah'll learn her thet men 'n women do the same. Fo' money? We-all have to pay plenty fo' stallions wut cover ourn mares."

"Leave it, Happy. Leave it."

"Nah. Buy thet mattress. Ah's goin' t'check on ourn Saudi prince's hosses."

Happy left me for the prince's double stalls. She had that look on her face that portends valuable meddling. My clairvoyant wife used her talents in many spheres.

Chapter 19

Happy got her way. She usually does.

The air mattress was duly installed in a squared-off area of our ample pantry.

When the following weekend rolled around, Basha collected her daughter from the autism place and brought her to our house.

Basha looked healthier, thanks to hearty meals with Bruno. She'd been given matching shoes by Happy, and an outfit from our local lightly-used shop that included pleated skirt, quilted windbreaker, and a woolen Peruvian-style cap. With her eyes alight, and wind-whipped pink cheeks, she was blossoming into a happier person.

Her "chile" was pretty but no outstanding drop-dead beauty. Dressed warmly but in an ugly grey uniform, she resisted all our attempts to rid her of moods. Her lips curved down, pouting permanently. Her eyes swiveled, with the pupils dilating. She let her tangled hair swing like a gypsy's.

Basha offered a succession of forced smiles.

After a big lunch, not made by Happy—thank Heavens—catered from town, we took the 'chile' to our stables for her initial introduction to babymaking.

Happy's first ploy was to introduce Anya to the kittens from Feathers' stall. Anya played with the kittens for most of an hour. Happy put an end to her playing by introducing a male cat to the kittens' mother, which happened to be in heat. A fact of which I'm damned sure Happy was well aware. That male cat proceeded to mount the female on schedule, while Anya looked on wide-eyed.

After that performance, Happy gave her plan a rest. A day later she led Anya to a nearby field, where the goat from Admiral Barge's stall was covering a newly arrived female goat, also in heat. I'm certain that the female was bought by Happy for the purpose of showing to Anya how goats mate.

The price of the goat duly appeared on my credit card's bill.

The next afternoon a rooster was on display rogering a hen. That was an easy inexpensive lesson because our farmyard was plentifully supplied with hens.

Finally Happy managed to bring Anya to have the very special experience of seeing a stallion covering a mare in season. By the time the afternoon was complete, Anya—reunited with a much admired kitten to take back to her air-mattress—was quite a changed little girl.

Giggling, Anya cuddled up to her mother. Like Timmy asking to go to McDonald's, she accompanied a request with a winsome smile: "Could go to ice-cream parlor, please?"

Mission accomplished, Happy packed our "chillun," Anya and Basha into our Volvo and headed for the nearest McDonald's.

Chapter 20

Anya never returned to "the autism place." Bruno leased a farm near ours, installed Basha and Anya there while he made preparations for a prompt wedding. Basha's papers were in order.

Happy provided flowers from Epsom's garden center, and paid for a wedding gown from the lightly-used shop.

The wedding was a delight. Basha asked Merrily to be her Matron of Honor. Anya was the flower girl, Tim her ring-bearer. I gave away the bride.

Tim was furious that the wedding breakfast took place in Epsom's finest restaurant, rather than in a McDonald's.

I got a little drunk.

There was no honeymoon. Not necessary. Bruno's sex problems had vanished.

Anya, entered into our local comprehensive school, where she made friends with another girl who liked kittens.

God was in his Heaven, and all was well in our world.

Until Bruno accepted to stand in at Covent Garden in Rossini's LE COMTE ORY. The booked male star, renowned for his Bel Canto renditions, had caught laryngitis. And it turned out that our main owner Fran Purcell was contracted to take the trouser role of Isolier in that opera: Bruno and Fran's characters competing for the on-stage love of Countess Adele.

Ouch.

Fran, never having forgiven Bruno for dumping her in favor of Nina, had refused to speak to him for the past year.

It was not going to be a jolly production.

As New York's Metropolitan Opera director, Bartlett Sher, famously said about opera: "a place where love is dangerous. People get hurt. That can be very funny and very painful. Rossini captures both—with the most beautiful music Rossini ever wrote."

For us, "dangerous" was the operative word.

Could I ever wipe from my mind memories of that terrible evening at La Scala? Immediately after ecstatic applause for Bruno's singing Qual Fiamma

Nel Guardo, he'd returned to his luxurious dressing room to learn that his Nina's dead body had been found and it had been disgustingly mutilated! I'd been grinding that scene in my mind for months, like a coffee plantation's roasting pans turn over a fire that's never put out.

I wasn't looking forward to LE COMTE ORY. Not that I expected murders and mutilated bodies on the scale of what we'd witnessed in Milan. The two evenings of that opera when we'd see it simply augured to be nasty.

We went to the Dress Rehearsal courtesy of pennypinching Fran. At that low-key performance we received chits for prima seats to the Opening Night, generously provided by Bruno.

Nothing terrible happened during the Dress Rehearsal.

Bruno had always had "five o'clock shadow" on his butting chin. It matched his coal-black hair. He really couldn't pass for a nun, which is essential for the male lead in LE COMTE ORY. Bruno kept a handkerchief to his chin and did his best to imitate the mincing walk of a young woman, but it didn't pass muster. I was hoping he'd get his pay check anyway in view of the superlative tones of his truly fine voice.

Fran did very well. Although most famous as a contralto, she was basically a mezzo-soprano, and knew her craft. As Isolier, her newly recaptured thin figure worked perfectly, and for Fran there'd been plenty of time for the wardrobe department to provide an ideal costume for her to pass as a man.

If only Merrily had stayed away from the Opening Night.

Chapter 21

Happy kept her distance when we saw Merrily sweep from her retro limo on to the sidewalk beyond the Covent Garden Opera House's side door. The newly refurbished premises had been given an extra-wide cement sidewalk interspersed with small trees. They were decorative, thanks to the sprouting of new leaves unfurling like swimming shrimps.

I felt amazed that Merrily would have chosen a side door when she always preferred to go where the paparazzi gathered. Publicity was so important to sales of her perfumes, cosmetics and face creams.

Merrily wore a floor length gown with a short fur wrap. Her shoes had fashionable five inch heels. Which she couldn't handle. One caught in the hem of her gown. She tripped. One heel broke off and sent a shoe flying. Merrily hit the sidewalk, hard.

Had she suffered a sprain on the foot missing the shoe? She couldn't stand up.

I darted forward to her, and tried to lift her. For that, I got punched in the ribs. When she recognized me she moaned 'hello' but continued to slap away my arms.

Attendants from the Opera House rushed to her and provided support. Were they worried she'd sue?

Merrily was ultra polite to these people, permitting them to bring her into the lobby where there were benches on either side of the front doors. She collapsed on a bench, patting it to indicate I was to sit beside her. She extended the shoeless foot, wiggled toes and rotated the ankle.

No harm done.

The shoe was recuperated. Merrily sat on the bench like a Cinderella being tested if the shoe fit. It did. Useless, however, because its heel had snapped away. Merrily would have had to hobble to her seat looking like a cripple who'd recently endured a knee operation.

Happy, always considerate of people, even those she didn't like, now appeared and offered her services to Merrily. "Ah knows this place. Ah c'n go past the Opery House's gift shop to an exit do'r where the Covent Garden shoppin' area have shoe stores. Wut be yourn size?"

Without a word to Happy, Merrily held out the broken shoe, indicating it would serve to provide her correct size. I handed my credit card to Happy, and she rushed into the side door and through the place where advance tickets could be collected. I watched her disappear beyond the exit to the shopping area.

Minutes later Happy returned with a pair of new shoes. Not chic. But they fit. Without thanks, Merrily let me slip on her shoes, and hurried to the Advance Tickets counter.

I shrugged, and returned my credit card to its slot in my wallet. After all, Merrily still had that fine colt in my stable.

It turned out that our courtesy tickets, offered by Bruno, were also at the Advance Tickets counter.

Merrily held a courtesy ticket in her hand. Next to her stood an exceedingly handsome younger man. He'd collected two tickets, one for himself and had given the other to Merrily.

She introduced him to us. "Meet John Doe. That isn't his real name, of course. But he uses it when he's with me because he works for a rival cosmetics company."

"Hi!" he extended a graceful hand. I noticed that it was manicured and a light colorless polish had been added to his nails. "Just call me Ioan. I can't have the paparazzi photograph me with Merrily because I'd get fired from my job. I work for a rival company." He grinned, showing off his capped teeth. He had a Romanian accent but a fair use of the English language. "Will you take her in to our seats?"

Happy warmed to Ioan. She grabbed the hand and pumped it like she would her old water outlet back home in Kentucky's hills.

Now we were stuck to escort Merrily into the orchestra area, like PT-boats convoying a battleship in dangerous seas.

Tough luck. Our seats were close to hers, in the same row. It meant that Merrily's new friend Ioan had also received complimentary tickets from a member of the cast or the Opera House's top echelon. She'd preferred to accept a comp ticket than buy one because the comp ticket had Ioan's name on the envelope.

We learned immediately from whom Ioan had received his.

Proudly, dropping her name like an avocado tree lets fall a ripe and greasy avocado, he showed off: "Our tickets came from THE Fran Purcell. You know, the world's greatest contralto, only tonight she's taken on the part of a mezzo-soprano."

And Merrily was Ioan's date? Oh, God! That meant Merrily was poaching, and on Fran's opera turf.

Not necessary for her to accept a "comp" ticket when Merrily's billion dollar company could well afford the best box in the Opera House!

What was going on? Merrily had never before shown us any raging desire for a man's attention. Why pick Fran's obvious choice? Fran would have received only two "comp" tickets. And while she could well afford to buy others, our pennypincher owner had used up these two on her new boyfriend, who'd passed on one of them to a woman that it was known she disliked.

Why?

The lights dimmed. Applause came like a wave to a beach as the orchestra's conductor approached the podium. Swoosh, the great curtains with their EII insignia revealed the backdrop for the first scene. A hush enveloped us.

For the initial strains of the overture we'd kept our eyes on the conductor. I had a habit of singling out the various instruments. I was looking for the oboe when a rustle of silk nearby caught my attention. Merrily was sneaking a hand to Ioan's fingers, encouraging them to work up higher from her knee.

Merrily saw me watching. She glared, but didn't remove her hand from guiding Ioan's.

Happy's glance had followed mine. Nothing new there. She'd observed Maheen's ex-courtesan mother work on our Canadian owner, using just that ploy.

Intermission interrupted the progression of his fingers to where she'd wanted them to arrive.

Four glasses of bubbly at Covent Garden prices! I didn't want to get stuck with the bill. Like an injured horse that trails at the back of a race, I followed her to the downstairs bar. For some reason she didn't want to climb the stairs to the grander premises where opera goers could sit at elegant tables. Maybe she did plan to pick up the bill, and hesitated to order food with the champagne, preferring to talk than to eat.

We found four seats on the long benches that snake the length of the walls on the lower level. Merrily took an end position, pulling Ioan down beside her, and placing me beyond Ioan, to keep Happy well away from him. Happy and I sipped our champagne in silence. Merrily chatted steadily to Ioan, not taking breath to interrupt praising the successes of her various products. "We're making billions, not just a billion!"

Ioan listened intently. Too intently. Was he going to quit his job with Merrily's competitor and aim for a higher salary as a traitor?

Where was Basha? She didn't appear for the Intermission, and hadn't had a comp ticket in line with ours.

When the third warning bell rang, we returned to our seats and I used my binoculars to scan the heads in rows ahead of ours. Nothing. No Basha.

I began to peruse the faces of people in the boxes closest to the stage, where blind spots prompted the management to give comp seats in them. Yes. Basha was in one on the right, cringing, looking scared again, and miserable.

Sitting beside her was Lord Cabrach, Fran's husband. He didn't seem very pleased, either. His wife had garnered enthusiastic applause. Bruno had reaped an ecstatic standing ovation.

Why were these two unhappy?

The answer developed at the end of the evening. After six curtain calls for the three principals, I felt I could discreetly head for home. I gave Happy a nod, but she was pointing to an elegant back in the front of the opera house. It belonged to Prince Mohammed Ben Saud, my new owner who was rapidly acquiring the best horseflesh in my stable by making offers no sane person would refuse. There was nothing for it but I'd have to delay our exit by greeting him respectfully.

Ben had no intention of being among the first of the audience to leave.

"Hello, Rick," he greeted me in his familiar style. And why not? He'd been part of our group when Happy had saved the life of President Sarkozy in Paris. "Didn't you think Fran was terrific? I'm going to wait in the lobby to congratulate her."

That meant I'd have to wait too.

Basha finally joined us because she wanted a ride back to our cottage in Epsom. Her Anya would need to be prepared for school early in the morning. Bruno had to remain in London for tomorrow's matinee' performance of LE COMTE ORY.

Basha skulked in the corner where ice cream was sold. Her face was contorted in a way that made me think of an internee of a concentration camp waiting to be led to a gas chamber. What could possibly cause her to be that frightened?

Merrily had tried to disappear. She'd opted to find her limo at the side entrance, determined not to be photographed with Ioan by those ever-lusting paparazzi.

Fran and Bruno joined us in the lobby. Fans rushed up to them begging for autographs or simply congratulating them on their singing. The two stars could have loitered in their rebuilt dressing rooms. The two-year remake of Covent Garden's Opera

House had been partly due to the fact that the old dressing rooms had leaked when it rained. Both Fran, and Bruno, were hungry for the adulation of their fans and went directly to mix with them.

To me, Fran gushed, "Did you notice that I was in great voice? I've sung that damned role so many times I know every word and how to make the acting work. So I could concentrate my all on producing the greatest sounds I'm capable of. Oh, it feels so wonderful that the performance is over, and I know I was in top form!"

Disaster!

Precisely when Fran was exulting about her voice, Ioan was caught between Merrily and Fran.

Immediately those two women behaved like hyenas fighting over a carcass. Forgetting to protect her singing voice, Fran screamed at Merrily. "You bitch, trying to steal my Ioan!"

Merrily abandoned her plan to avoid the paparazzi and retaliated with blasts of hatred, "Not yours, you rapacious whore!"

Agonizing near them were Jeremy, and Basha. Two utterly devastated victims of the women's lust for Ioan.

I made my move. I circled an arm around Basha's curving back and drew her outside. I'd been lucky to park my car near the front entrance on the opposite side of the street. With Happy like a tug boat leading us forward, we avoided oncoming traffic, reached the car and sped away.

We were on the M-25 before I learned what had terrorized Basha,

Happy leaned toward me and whispered, "Basha done told me that Ioan had been one of her payin' Johns. He got real dirty idees. Whipped her. 'N worse. Cain't tell Bruno, no way. Bruno could kill Ioan fo' wut he done."

Really? I doubted Bruno would go to such an extreme. Romanians in exile stuck together, even sex rivals. There was a Romanian Mafia of sorts that guaranteed protection to many exiles.

Chapter 22

Happy's comment regarding Ioan rang loud in my memory when a week past and there was no further sign of Ioan.

He seemed to have disappeared from all known venues. A man who'd texted Fran daily never sent another text. Nothing on his Facebook. No Twitters. Where was he? I'd informed Scotland Yard. Jeremy, although he despised the man, got his former colleagues in M15 to put a trace on Ioan.

Decent of Jeremy, considering he knew his wife had been having an affair with the man.

When there's a murder, there's usually a body. Could he have been incinerated? Or his body dumped down a well and acid thrown in after him to obliterate all trace of his murder? Like the Bolsheviks had done to Romanovs in Ekaterinaburg?

"He ain't daid," Happy told me solemnly ten days after Ioan's disappearance. She and I had perched on our bumwarmer enjoying the heat from our fireplace on an evening when the weather dipped again to below freezing. We could hear Basha still upstairs with Anya, preparing her child for bed. Anya shared the master bedroom with Basha when Bruno was on tour. Bruno's outstanding success in LE COMTE ORY at Covent Garden had harvested three engagements on the Continent to reprise the role in minor opera houses. "Ioan be too valu'ble."

What Happy meant by that remark I wasn't to know.

The early flat racing had begun at Ascot. All my attention had to be concentrated on our stable to select any among our equine stars that could give peak performances. The trick was to race those which truly ached to be out competing and know which horses should be kept back to be totally ready.

Ben had left for his principality. He disliked the return to low temperatures and wouldn't appear again until Royal Ascot's balmier weather. But he hadn't left without managing to buy our favorite colt in my stable and finalizing the paper work to acquire Merrily's colt for a price that even she had not refused. Goodbye Merrily from our stable!

<>

139

Lucky for me. I had less pressure pulluting the pleasant atmosphere of my tack-room-cum-office. I could fully concentrate on making entries for my most forward future champions.

Weeks later, when my most favorite of race meetings hit the calendar, I duly did my best to measure up to what could be accomplished there. And after Ben's best colt won at Royal Ascot, I received his trophy from the gloved hands of my Monarch.

Queen Elizabeth's love for racing hadn't diminished, even with the renewed pressures on her reign. Again she had kind words for my Happy, saying in her cut crystal voice: "You are doing well, Mrs. Harrow."

Fran's best filly won a prize too, but on that day Her Majesty's work had been really too pressing for an added appearance in the winner's circle. Her Majesty had often referred to "Working above the store." That day she'd left Royal Ascot races and Windsor Castle for a "working tea" in Buckingham Palace.

Those wins were followed by one at Newbury and another at Kempton. I took some of our minor runners to Beverley and to York, but they weren't good enough and came in Second and Third.

On the afternoon of a hot summer's day our Head Lad, Tom, strolled into my tack room-cum-office. "Mr. Harrow, Sir," he began very formally, "I've heard a whisper that Sir Benjamin Slade of Maunsel, in Somerset, might want to have a horse trained by yourself."

"Oh? Thank you, Tom. You know that's better than music to my ears. Tell me more."

"Sir Benjamin, he be brother-in-law to that Lord Rotherwick what won the Irish Oaks, and then he also took Ascot's Queen Elizabeth II Stakes with HOMING."

"I'm not about to forget *him.*"

"No, Sir. I been sure o' thet. Well, this here Sir Benjamin Slade, he made a fortune in containers for them big cargo ships. He also gets him fifty thousand visitors to his Maunsel house every year, payin' God knows what. Got hisself famous fo' winnin' a legal case for to keep his dog"

"I certainly recall that too."

"Sir Benjamin Slade used to have a cattery. Invited females to visit a prime stud cat his wife owned."

"Can certainly afford to buy a damned fine horse."

"He be a lucky owner. Yes, Sir. I grew up in Somerset. I think, but I may be wrong, that Maunsel were famous when I was a lad. Was supposed to have been a murder there. One of them jealousy cases."

"That seems more like Mrs. Harrow's line of country."

"Yes, Sir. It were in them Edwardian days when ladies still wore corsets. Took place during a weekend when guests come to shoot pheasants. Later at night, a lot of scurryin' from one bedroom to another or to men's dressin' rooms. One guest, known to be extremely jealous of his pretty, but flirtatious wife, kept his beady eye on a fellow guest who got her eyelids flutterin'. On the second day of shootin' them pheasants there be no sign of the fellow. The husband was in the line all right, but not the other fellow. Never seen again. Anywheres. Seems like the husband found that his wife's corset strings had been cut with a scissors. Her lady's maid had quit thet mornin' and the husband fumed that it was thet fellow who had cut her corset strings fo' ye-know-wut."

I growled. "I never was one to like those shooting parties where most of the men were prowling for other men's wives rather than aiming at pheasants."

"Sir, I may be wrong. Perhaps it weren't at Maunsel, but at another of them great Somerset houses. Give Sir Benjamin Slade a bell on the blower to invite him to your stables."

"Thanks, Tom. I will." It was a fruitless call. Sir Benjamin Slade was too busy arranging for wedding parties to hire Maunsel. He didn't bother to return the message I'd left on his answering machine. Oh, well. That's par for the course for Trainers.

I was toiling in my tack-room-cum-office, studying the season's racing calendar to make summer entries for our string, when the telephone rang. I still made more use of telephones than texting or e-mails.

A garbled voice groaned, "Turkey. Save me. I'm in Turkey." Click. End of call.

Wrong number?

No.

When Happy joined me several minutes later, her cell phone rang. With her delicious behind perched on my desk, Happy clicked on the caller. I recognized the same frenzied, desperate voice.

Happy said, "How c'n Ah help? Ah's in England. Ain't got money fo' to go t'Turkey. Don't rightly knows where-all thet be. Sorry."

The voice pleaded on.

With no obvious regret, Happy explained: "Ah's got chillun to care fo' and there be hosses to ready fo' Summer Ascot. Cain't just catch an air-plane. Sorry."

Sobs intermingled with more despairing pleas.

Shrugging her slim shoulders, Happy ended: "Gimme the ad-dress. Ah's goin' to see wut-all Ah'll do." Happy turned off her cell phone, wrote down an address, left my desk and paced the tiny tack room. "Thet be Ioan. Not daid. Not yet. Went to thet Turkey hopin' to get a humongous fee. Didn't get no fee, just had his knuckles broke. 'N his nose. Won't be so handsome."

"Not dead. That's something. But he's such a nasty piece of work. Didn't you tell me he'd whipped Basha, and hurt her other ways?"

"Basha done tole me thet. Ah's no rea-son t'doubt her. Ioan be kinky. Disgustin'. But he ain't no murderer."

"No."

"Ah thinks as Ah knows who be doin' the killin's o' folks in ourn circle. Thet person won't stop at flushin Ioan down t'Hell. He cain't count fo' much. Get a bullet in the head once he cain't make up he knows anythin' mo'e. Rick-honey, Ah's goin' t'call Maheen. She be Muslim. Could get around Turkey. Understands them folks."

I shook my head. "Maheen won't want to leave behind her baby, and Luca."

"Mebbe they go with her. Won't hurt none t'call."

Happy knew Maheen's number. No need to look in the Directory. Within seconds I could hear Maheen's cheerful voice.

After a series of exclamations regarding Maheen's baby, Happy made her pitch.

Maheen didn't like it. "Happy, Luca's in Turkey. Dangerous place. The Islamist government there has just released prisoners from all its jails. Some kind of amnesty. Honest people are adding extra locks to their doors. Keeping children at home. My husband has been seconded to Istanbul's police force to study the situation."

"Yippee! Then y'all don't mind goin' there. Leave yourn baby in Lake Garda with the grandma."

"I could. Luca has been urging me to come to Istanbul. But I'm not mixing up in this Ioan business unless you come too!"

Silence at Happy's end.

Maheen pressed on. "I'll ask Hal to cover our expenses. He's such a great step-father. I know this isn't going to put a dent in the Murphy fortune, and he'll say yes."

Chapter 23

Hal did. Always the most generous owner in my stable, he'd ante-ed up the cash when Happy was abducted in Dubai, when Tim was kidnapped in Kentucky, and had personally gone after the Mexican hitman to pay the gangster who'd grabbed his wife Mafalda.

This time his money came with strings attached. Hal insisted on flying to Istanbul with Mafalda. He liked Luca Palacio, but wasn't going to let him be solely responsible for Maheen's safety.

With Hal on board, I agreed that Happy could leave our "chillun," horses, and me for a week. I placed myself at the bottom of Happy's love-'em totem pole.

Seven days. The initial twenty-four hours went into packing her gear, joining Maheen at Rome's Airport, and settling in at a former palace, now the Giragan Palace Kempenski Hotel. Together with the Senior Murphys, Happy relaxed enjoying the view of the Bosporus before she could get a trace on Ioan.

Happy had corralled Jeremy Cabrach's MI5 friends for aid in tracking Ioan's whereabouts. MI5 had taken an interest in Ioan's disappearance.

MI5 had the most sophisticated technology available. Ioan's last address proved helpful. Within hours of Happy's request she was given valuable information.

He'd been held in a fairly comfortable house in the Alkent Sitesi neighborhood on Tepecik Street, not exactly an affluent residential area, but quiet and unassuming-enough not to draw attention to what was going on.

Maheen, as she'd done before, was quick at discovering the reason for Ioan's abduction. Cozying up to the Muslim housekeeper at Number 22, Ataturk, Maheen learned that by eavesdropping daily the housekeeper overheard Ioan giving some details of a new facecream product guaranteed to erase wrinkles.

"Lutfen, please tell me more."

"His company had a secret formula." A competing corporation had salivated for it, and BINGO weak Ioan had supplied parts of the nitty-gritty. But he'd wanted big money from the rival firm. It hadn't been forthcoming. Dissatisfied with the small amount of cash received, Ioan had withheld the formula's essential ingredients, and the missing chemical mix. Which was the reason for having his knuckles and nose broken.

"Tesekkur ederim," Maheen breathed. She learned that Ioan had been spirited away from Etoiler's Tepecik yolu.

The spying housekeeper hadn't been able to find out where he'd gone. She had one additional piece of information. She added the fact that Ioan was a diabetic and needed insulin shots twice daily. Without them Ioan would die without any need to shoot him. According to the sneaky housekeeper, Ioan had been supplied with insulin during the entire time he was in Istanbul.

Maheen added: "That woman thinks the kidnappers took him south to Kusadasi. To Ephesos."

Hal interrupted. "Been there, done the touring. That's a great place for you to see, Happy. If you remember your Bible, you'll recall that Saint Paul addressed the Ephesians there, and wrote an Epistle to them. You'll walk on the same cobblestones that

Saint Paul walked on, if you go to Ephesos. Personally, I was intrigued there'd been a brothel there in Saint Paul's time."

Mafalda, not pleased to be reminded of a brothel in words that reeked of knowledge of her courtesan era, now frowned: new wrinkles made, or no new wrinkles made. "Hal! I will not go to Kusadasi."

"My dear, you need not go. You can read all aboot it in our guide book."

Maheen didn't want her mother to rumble into a rage. She was disturbed on hearing Hal's first innuendo of a sneer to her mother. Did it mean that Hal and Mafalda's long honeymoon was over? "I'll go to Kusadasi. Maybe I can get Luca to come too. Or you, Happy."

Happy, who was eating a baklava cake, put down her fork. "All three of usn should go."

She hadn't felt keen about leaving Istanbul before exploring its ancient sites. Happy's ongoing fascination for 'old stones' hadn't yet been satisfied. She'd explored the former Santa Sofia Cathedral, now a major mosque, and visited the Topaki Museum. The Four Seasons Hotel had been a former palace, but none of those places were ancient enough to interest my archeolgy-minded Happy.

Maheen got the go-ahead from Luca, Hal was waved off by Mafalda. With Happy as the Third Musketeer they set out for the domestic flights' airport for their trip to Kusadasi.

At Kusadasi they had to make another decision. Which village should they scour for Ioan? Maheen judged Ephesus too well-known. "Those kidnappers don't want to be noticed."

Happy suggested Selcuk. "Ah's read about thet town on Google. Only twenty minutes from Kusadasi. Big with tourists. Lots o' them men in Panama hats 'n ladies in shorts. We uns knows thet the kidnappers won't want no way to stand out as Englishmen in Saville Row clothes. Plenty other Englishmen in Selcuk in shorts, tourin.'"

Maheen said: "Selcuk. Good choice. We can join up with a group on a tour bus. Won't be noticed on our arrival if we come with a group of English tourists. After we've arrived we'll have to find a nondescript taxi to check out the pharmacies that provide insulin."

Hal paid for a round trip tour in order to put off any suspicion.

On the bus, Hal cozied up to a couple of tourists from Canada. He'd recognized their Nova Scotia Maritime accents.

"What about tourist attractions?" he asked in his booming voice, establishing that the three newcomers were also touring.

The Canadian wife spoke out for both of them. Her tones were shrill enough for the tour guide to hear every word. "We make a stop at the hot springs of Pamukkale. Short one. None of our group voted to try those springs. Too many sick people using them. Might catch something nasty."

Happy chimed in: "What about arch-i-tect-ural sites? Ah loves old stones."

The Canadian husband wanted to show off his knowledge of digs. His Maritime accent was even more pronounced than his wife's. "Plenty of those. Aboot every village on our route shows off some stones dug up nearby."

His wife wasn't going to shut up. She sent her shrilling tones to the bus driver. "I hope we stop in Loy. The village's name means cherry blossoms in Turkish, because that village specializes in growing cherry trees. With any luck some of the trees will still be in flower."

The three Musketeers weren't to know. They slipped away from the tour group as soon as their bus settled at a comfort stop in Selcuk. Hal made a detour past the Men's Toilets, and joined Happy and Maheen at the taxi rank.

Maheen had already picked out a seedy, rusting taxi. Hal went up front with the driver. Happy and Maheen took the back seat where there were curtains for the windows. They quickly drew those blinds while Hal gave instructions in Canadian French to tell the driver to take him to the largest pharmacy in Selcuk.

The taxi was filthy inside. Maheen and Happy's legs were threatened by cockroaches. "Do them bite, yo'all think?" Happy queried, raising her toes as high as her knees.

"Wouldn't think so. We've got plenty of cockroaches in Egypt. And they don't bite."

Booming noise filled the taxi from the driver's two-way radio. When it wasn't blaring outdated jazz, the radio bleated out addresses of expectant passengers. The driver replied on the return frequency, barking what was indistinguishable for the three Musketeers.

Maheen ventured, "I think he said he'd already got passengers. Referred to us as Canadians."

Their taxi stopped at a large pharmacy. Hal hurried inside. He returned looking downcast. "Won't sell insulin without a doctor's prescription. Won't say if any Englishmen have asked for some."

The taxi driver skirted along the Aegean shore to find a second pharmacy. This time it was Maheen who asked for information about insulin in the shop. Her face was alight when she climbed back into her seat.

"I questioned the pharmacist about insulin. He said there were two Englishmen who picked up a supply of insulin every day. They had a prescription, but only for a small amount. The men are due to arrive any moment."

Careful not to pay the taxi in case it would abandon them, the three Musketeers told the driver to wait and proceeded to locate a suitable hiding place. They chose the local garden center because it was filled with foreigners. The local Turks didn't waste shopping money on flowers.

"Lookee what a contrast in this here village," Happy observed. "There come a Rolls Royce with its chauffeur deliverin' kids to go waterskiin', and on thet same road be a donkey loaded with firewood led by a peasant. Po'r man, he ain't got no shorts to wear like all these toorists. Probably same tattered trousers summer or winter."

Hal interrupted. "Happy, you love old stones. Look away from the seashore, fine ancient columns to your left. The village elders must have gone to some trouble to display their antiquities. But there's not really much. What's left of pillars, and a stone bench. Could date from Alexander The Great's time."

He was interrupted in his turn when a battered mini-cooper belched its way to the pharmacy and disgorged the two English kidnappers. In an attempt to blend in with the crowds of tourists they were outfitted in garish shorts from the local market. But their Turnbull & Asher long-sleeved shirts were a give away that these two Brits belonged in an elegant office in London.

They scurried into the pharmacy, where they made a quick purchase and soon scurried back to their mini-cooper. At the sound of their motor being revved, the three Musketeers rushed to their taxi and Hal gave the time-battered order: "Follow that car."

The mini-cooper's driver was careful not to break any speed limits. It dawdled at every stop sign and its driver gave a wanna-be-friendly thumbs up to the town's one traffic policeman.

Hal's taxi was filthy but its driver was well-versed in keeping a viable distance when in pursuit of a prey. The driver must have spent many a fruitful day hunting hares for his table.

The mini-cooper's driver adroitly flashed a red signal when pulling up to a run down hut, advising he was about to stop. He let out his passenger, then smoothly skirted the hut to mask the mini-cooper behind a large tree with branches tumbling down like a graceful willow.

A door slammed shortly after.

The passenger had stooped to collect a bottle of milk from the front entrance, and carried the milk inside. Although sunlight shone as brightly as fireworks, sending piercing rays to dive through the tree's branches, an electric light bulb was switched on from deep within the hut.

A horrific scream erupted into the calm afternoon.

Gasps came like bullets, then sobs from a man's heavy weeping.

In one great leap Happy surged toward the front entrance.

Not allowed. Hal produced interference like a football player from McGill University. Shaking his huge head, he added a finger to his lips to demand silence and obedience. Maheen nodded. She'd understood the need for care in this dread place. Happy's attempt at heroism had to be postponed.

Following the example of the mini-cooper's driver, Hal slunk around the hut to reach its back door. He tried it.

Locked.

Maheen gestured to Happy to tiptoe into the patio and do a search.

With Hal playing goal-keeper, Maheen and Happy tested the area for hidden booby traps. They found none. What they did find was a weathered last-century water pump. Made of iron, it dominated a corner of the patio.

Happy whispered, "We'uns had a pump like this one in mah ole home in Kentucky. Let me see if'n it works."

It did. Happy plied her know-how to its heavy handle. Out poured a mighty gush of rust-colored water. Like lava from a volcano it burst into the afternoon heat, towering over the hut.

Hal said, "We had a pump like this one in a mining camp when I was a youngster. As I recall, the head comes off, and that head could provide one hell of a useful weapon." He fiddled with its worn screws and off came the head accompanied by a brook-sized stream of water. The patio soon became a wading pool, with its corner tiles serving to capture the overflow.

A squeak from the patio door announced it was being opened. Hal positioned himself to one side of it.

The mini-cooper's driver appeared, wearing a very startled expression. Hal changed the look on the man's face very quickly by banging him with the head of the pump. Down went that kidnapper. His face had turned ashen, with rivulets of blood tracing a spider web pattern.

The second kidnapper called out, "What the hell?" He was armed with a shotgun.

He peered into the patio, more cautious than his bull-headed partner. When he saw that his partner was lying prone face down in a foot of water, he still hesitated. He sensed rather than saw the Musketeers.

Happy didn't wait for him to brandish his shotgun with its engraved Purdy stock resting with pride of place in his palm. Like a fer-de-lance she covered ten feet in seconds to swoop down on him and pull him into the foot-high water. Her hair and clothes soaked, Happy held that kidnapper as if she was reining in a rogue horse near the Finish Line. Crash went the shotgun, drowned in the patio's foot deep water.

A splashing bout followed. Nobody winning. Tiny Happy, the right size for a jockey but hardly equal to dominating a six-foot-Brit, was being pummeled mercilessly. Hal strode over as if on a stage and down came the water pump's handle. No mercy given. The second kidnapper now lay face-down in the rising water.

Whimpering from inside the hut alerted the Musketeers that they must go to Ioan.

With the bloodied water pump in hand, Hal stood over the two kidnappers while Maheen and Happy explored the hut's interior. The hut, which had looked small from the street, was more adequate than they could have guessed. There was a shuttered room for artillery, with two Italian-make grenades, a machine gun, and boxes of cartridges. These were positioned on what had been a billiard table.

Two other rooms had beds and bureaus, but no sheets on the beds. Open drawers revealed the bureaus were empty.

A kitchen brought sneers from Maheen/ "Even in a hovel there's better in Egypt," she declared.

The sound of her voice brought renewed whimpering from a storage room. Happy and Maheen opened its door to reveal a windowless shelved room obviously intended for maturing cheeses. A short cot contained Ioan, whose broken nose had nothing better than a bandaid on it, while his broken hands had no bandages at all. The injury on his nose was badly infected.

Smelly pus oozed from it.

"Hi, yo'all," Happy went eyeball to eyeball with the kidnappers' victim. "Ioan, this lady be Maheen, who done helped me on other cases. Yo'all got t'git up ofn thet there cot 'n come with usn, quick-like. But first, yo'all got a towel? Ah's mighty wet."

Ioan attempted a nod in Maheen's direction. He sat up and gestured to a towel rack that contained one much-bloodied towel.

Happy didn't hesitate to use it. She worked it over her mud-flattened yellow curls. Meanwhile, unabashed by Ioan's staring eyes, Maheen removed her T-shirt to offer it to Happy.

Maheen's jacket, buttoned up, served to cover her breasts.

Eyeing a pair of rusted scissors, Happy cut her jeans to the size of tourists' shorts. She gave a drying swipe to her sandals, and led the way to the front door.

There, Maheen yelled out for their taxi driver to collect them. In Turkish, she ordered him to use his two-way radio to call for police.

Waiting for the police, Hal remained in the patio, standing guard over the kidnappers.

Amazingly, a policeman arrived within minutes. Hal watched him manacle the two kidnappers, then stood by while the two Englishmen were caged in by bars in the rear of his vehicle. Both men were still out of it, unaware that they'd been arrested and their game was over.

Their taxi driver had made sure that the local policeman realized he hadn't been called out on an ordinary fight between foreigners. The taxi driver displayed Ioan's wounds for the policeman to see, while Maheen continued to show off her knowledge of Turkish by telling the policeman that his two prisoners were would-be killers who'd been hired to dispose of Ioan.

The Selcuk police car sped off with its regulation rooftop light flashing in time-honored form. The policeman didn't bother to wave at the Musketeeers.

With his four passengers the taxi driver skirted the Aegean beaches, describing them in the tones of a Selcuk tour guide although none of the four could care less.

Always the generous guy, Hal gave him an over-the-top tip when they were deposited at the Kusadasi Airport.

"Ah sho hopes he be usin' thet money to rid his cab o' cockroachs," Happy purred.

Maheen retorted, "Don't talk cockroachs now. I'm starving and want to go into the nearest watering hole to fill my tummy. I'm hoping *that* place's kitchen will be free of all vermin. Rats, included."

Happy and Maheen selected the airport restaurant as if they were on a shopping spree at Harvey Nicks, heading for its famous top floor.

Hal and Ioan chose to go into the Men's Lavatories to clean up and exchange information.

After inquiring as to Ioan's state of health, and commiserating over his broken nose and knuckles, Hal said, "I'll wager the Selcuk policeman turned over his two captive Englishmen for the local magistrate to deal with. Then he'd take for himself the credit for subduing them with the top of an iron pump."

Causing the loose pus-filled bandaid on his nose to fall off, Ioan said, "Just count yourself lucky you weren't charged for the damage to the water pump."

When the two men joined Happy and Maheen at a table for four, Maheen said, "We don't want to have to face a local Turkish magistrate ourselves on some trumped-up charge. Happy could be had up for assault and battery. You, too, Hal."

"Because of what *we* did to the kidnappers?" Hal queried. "What times we live in! How'd *you* get mixed up with them, Ioan? Not funny, having your nose and knuckles broken. I suppose they deserve whatever torture the locals deal out. I recall that in Peter O'Toole's Lawrence of Arabia movie, Lawrence got tortured by his Turkish captors."

Touching his face using wrists only, Ioan whimpered, "Bag men. Supposed to bring me an incredible amount of money offered in exchange for a chemical formula for my company's experimental facecream. The kidnappers are highly-paid executives of a rival company. Didn't you notice they wore Saville Row shirts and club ties?"

"I noticed. What about the shotgun one of them had?"

"It belonged to the exec who accompanied me from London. He got it through airport security due to a letter he produced inviting him to go game shooting in Turkey. But when I was moved to that squalid hut, I knew the plan was to blast my head full of bird shot once the second man got the formula."

"Did he?"

"No. Not all of it."

"You'll have to go undercover when you return to England."

"No. Go to the nearest hospital. Can't wait for Londons'. These knuckles have got to be dealt with fast or I'll lose the use of my hands. And my nose? God, I'm going to look ugly with a broken nose. Needs a plastic surgeon at least."

"People get shot in hospitals."

"Won't you and your wife be returning to Italy? Could I get off the plane in Rome with you?"

Hal agreed to that plan. Not enthusiastically, but for humanitarian reasons.

There was no need for Ioan to say 'xopowwee noka' to Kusadasi.

Their airplane left on time. Maheen had texted Luca and he was at their Istanbul destination with bunches of flowers for Happy and Maheen. He gave Hal welcoming slaps on the back.

Ioan, he ignored.

While Luca went to the Air Italia counter to change the date for the return journey to Rome, Happy and Maheen explored the tourism office's shelves of pamphlets describing archeological sites to visit.

Maheen squealed with pleasure. "I'd like to go to all of them. I'd even go on to Armenia to poke around the place where they've just discovered the oldest wine bottles in existence. No, the bottles are not in Israel, as had been thought. Armenia."

Luca joined them in time to stop that plan. "Maheen darling, you must want to hurry back to our little girl. But I'll agree to exactly ONE archeological dig. Take your pick. I'll need some time tomorrow with the Istanbul police."

Decisions, decisions. Happy's great at making them where murders are concerned. It wasn't that easy for her to influence Maheen to go to the place she'd been longing to see.

"Ah's leanin' toward goin' to find Armina's island prison. Ain't she be the sor-cer-ess wut got all them men to stay there with her?"

Maheen hooted. "That's just a legend, Happy. Operas written about it. Sure, by Haydn, Rossini, Gluck and Dvorak. Doesn't mean there was any such island. No, I suggest we follow the trail of Alexander The Great and see one of the cities he built on his travels. He started out in Macedonia, got to Egypt, but died somewhere near where we were yesterday. Wonderful old stones for you to explore."

"Thet be the Alexander wut cut the Gordeon Knot! Thet no one had been able to untie?"

"The same. Happy, I guarantee you'll love any city he built. Selcuk had a mere few fragments."

Maheen picked the right place. With merely four hours to delve deeply into the ruins, what with having spent most of the next day in airplanes to reach them, Happy was contented if not satiated.

She would have liked to get off in Rome and wander around *its* ancient ruins, but when Maheen and Luca left their flight with Ioan in tow, Happy had barely minutes to make her connection to London. Hal and Mafalda had opted to remain in Italy. Still honeymooning? Who was to know!

Of all the four million passengers that crowd through London's Heathrow Airport each day, Happy recognized only one face. Merrily was at the Air Italia counter, booking a seat to Rome.

Chapter 24

When Happy was cozily perched on our bumwarmer back home in Epsom, she told me, itemized, everything that had happened on her trip. All the conversations. She described facial expressions. Everything. She was mystified by Merrily's appearance booking a flight to Rome, but had a comment on that, too.

"Ah's reservin' my opinion, but it do seem she booked to where Ioan went: awful quick-like."

Our Richard wanted to show off how well he'd learned to walk and started tumbling too close to the fireplace. When Happy picked him up in her arms, she noticed that he had a fever.

Again our Epsom pediatrician suggested we take Richard to the Great Ormond Street Children's Hospital in London. Happy bundled him in his winter clothes although it was spring, and I drove them to the hospital.

Addison's disease! Richard was diagnosed as having the same curse that hounded President John F. Kennedy all through his youth and political career. The young Jack had been submitted to terrible tests all through his early days. It was when his father became U.S. Ambassador to the Court of St. James. and the family had moved to London, that Jack Kennedy's Addison's disease was discovered.

A white-coated doctor told me and Happy that little Richard needed an abdominal x-ray, a CT scan, arteriography, radionuclide scanning, and IV scanning of the kidneys before he could decide whether or not our Richard had a truly serious case of the disease.

"But wut be this-here disease. Wur-all cause it?"

A bleak look washed over the doctor's creased face. "In the majority of cases Addison's is caused by an autoimmune attack on the adrenal glands."

Uh. I understood, but I'm not sure that my Happy did.

Surprise! Happy not only understood, but she had a cure for the problem. "In Kentucky, we'uns give licorice to ourn sick folks with ad-re-nal failures."

"You're right, Mrs. Harrow. Pure, real licorice is one of the cures recommended for a light case of Addison's. Pure licorice, not a commercial brand that contains no real licorice. It helps to reduce the amount of hydrocortisone broken down by the liver, thereby reducing the work loads of the adrenal glands. Best to give it in teas or supplements. But there's a down side to using licorice. Long term use can be very harmful. Daily use of more than ten grams is not advised. Excessive use can cause water retention and increased blood pressure."

"Dear God, no!" I resolved not to let Happy ply her Kentucky cure without supervision by a qualified doctor.

We checked in to an upscale Bed & Breakfast in Kensington. With our Head Lad detailed to oversee the morning and evening gallops, that imperative job was taken care of. It was the readying of my Royal Ascot runners that gave me the greatest concern, yet little Richard's survival certainly had priority and we stayed in town until all the gruesome tests were completed.

Yes, no doubt about it. Our little Richard had a mild case of Addison's. The tests had decisively proved it.

Even mild Addison's required expert physician intervention and supervision. That would require years of trips to London, with more overnight stays. Never mind, that would be done.

Glucocorticoid and mineralcorticoid drugs were prescribed. Would National Health pay for any of that, or would my diminishing financial reserves go?

DHEA was added to the list of helpful drugs. It was expected to suppress any inflammatory cytokines and down-regulate autoimmune reactions in little Richard's body.

Forget cost! I knew I'd run out of what we'd put aside for my retirement. So what? The answer must be to win big races with ten percent of the prizes to go to our stable.

* * *

We made a fine start. We won valuable purses at Newbury and at Kempton. We'd held in reserve two of our speediest colts and they did very well indeed at Ascot's summer races.

Never gloat. I was on Cloud Nine in my Tack Room, gloating what success we'd had at summer Ascot, and the telephone rang.

Bruno's Romanian accent colored the glorious tenor tones that wafted from my receiver. "Found him! The you-know-who some guys had sequestered from the Italian hospital, and took to where-I-cannot-say on telephone. Meet me tonight eight o'clock French time, at Charles De Gaulle Airport, Paris of course, outside Maxim Restaurant. I have tickets for the you-must-not-say-on-telephone place."

My mind quickly filled in the dots. Bruno had heard that Ioan had been grabbed from the Italian hospital, and taken somewhere else. "Can I bring my wife?" I asked.

"Sure. Bring your Happy. She always great help."

"Happy won't come without the three kids."

I heard Bruno sigh. "Kids, too. I get five more tickets. See you at restaurant."

Sprinting out of the Tack Room, barefooted because I'd removed my riding boots, I hurried home. "Happy, pack up. We're leaving in ten minutes. Take only the essentials for the kids. Bruno has news. Ioan's been kidnapped by associates of those bastards whom Hal clobbered in Turkey. Bruno knows where he is. I guessed you'd want to accompany me to locate him."

"Yo'all got thet right. Ten minutes? Ah's gonna make it in five."

She did. Into the Volvo I packed her and the kids and all their usual gear. We headed at full speed, just under the limit, to reach Heathrow in time for the late flight to Paris.

Bruno, tapping a patent leather shoe as he stared in the wrong direction, was lurking next to the main door of the Charles de Gaulle Airport Maxim Restaurant.

We slapped each other's shoulders. A hug for Happy. Bruno messily kissed my two youngest children, but Tim had been too quick to be caught for one of his garlic kisses.

"Rick, we go San Remo."

No time to eat at the restaurant. The six of us dashed to the starting gate for a flight to San Remo. Happy had to carry baby Richard, who would have dragged us back if he'd tried toddling, and so when I say six of us, that meant Richard dashing in Happy's arms.

Happy's over-weight baby-gear caused a brief set-back. Bruno got around it by flashing the six tickets and claiming each of the six tickets had carry-on rights.

It was midnight when we arrived in downtown San Remo, and found our 1920's-style GRANDE EPOQUE hotel. No way were we going to be able to see Ioan that same day.

Happy had gone on strike. She needed to feed and bathe the "chillun."

It was the next morning before we got organized to rent a Fiat to head for the hills to try to rendezvous with Ioan. And then there was a delay while Happy found a babysitter. She hit gold. That meant a really nice woman contracted by the hotel, who duly located a park for the "chillun" with swings and roundabouts. We duly parked the "chillun" there with the babysitter.

"Ioan not in Italy. He in Menton. That is France," Bruno stated flatly. "I have Romanian friend who willing hide Ioan in convalescent center he run outside Menton. But he no want trouble. I promise no trouble. So we fly Italy to put off any baddies following us."

Soon we crossed what had been the border between Italy and France, before the European Union abolished borders. We entered the frontier town, Menton, after driving through Veintimiglia.

Happy cooed, "Ah seen this place in thet ole' movie DAY OF THE JACKAL, when thet ass-a-sin hid the rifle in his muffler."

Bruno, sleep-deprived and nervous about the coming encounter, snapped, "We not touring. Look ahead. In the far hills be great gardens. Empress Eugenie owned one in Nineteenth Century. We go past it to Englishman Mr. Waterman's place. He has moon door to catch view of Menton. We not look. We go straight to my friend."

The convalescent center was housed in a magnificent mid-Nineteenth Century Garnier mansion. Garnier, one of my favorite mid-Nineteenth Century architects, who designed the Paris Opera House, as well as Monte Carlo's, all of which we'd visited, also knew how to create charming homes. Menton had a spread of them.

This house was resplendent with extra architectural details, inlaid tiles, small columns, a skylight, and mini statues gracing corners. Ioan's room was hideous. Hospital-plain, it was painted in bile green and stripped of anything that could possibly harvest germs, a virus, or bacteria.

Ioan was sitting up in bed. To my horror I counted only one leg. What had happened to the other one?

His face was bandaged, but I'd expected that because I knew his nose had been broken. Both hands were wrapped in plaster of paris. He waved enthusiastically with both of them. Through his bandages he snuffled, "Bruno, Rick, and Happy! I, who no visitors have had, now have a garden of visitors." He had forgotten current English, and regressed into what he must have learned in his Romanian college.

Bruno tried to kiss Ioan, but that proved difficult with so many bandages. He garbled some words in Romanian, then switched to English for our benefit.

"My Romanian friends, like a Mafia, get Ioan away from bastards what cut off his right leg. Not both legs. They wanted him know how much pain and misery is, when lose one leg, so he talk and tell formula or bastards cut off left leg."

Happy, who'd seen so many shockers during her career as a sleuth, went pale. She started shuddering. I placed an arm around her shoulders for comfort, but it was Ioan who managed to bring back a smile.

Ioan hadn't lost the sense of humor he'd earlier displayed in Turkey in the miserable hut where he'd been sequestered and had his nose and his knuckles broken. He winked at Happy, "Not a nose for a nose this time! Bad men threatened to cut off the left leg, the only one I have now, if not give complete formula. So I give them formula, complete. But I not tell how the ingredients must be combined. Ha, ha. I keep left leg. When I find woman missing right leg we can fit together to make the love!"

Happy winked in return. I sensed she still didn't like Ioan as a person. He earned commiseration, that was all. Or did she suspect Ioan of the murders that had taken place in Palm Beach, London, and Monte Carlo?

She had discarded that idea in a trice after one look at his mutilated body. "Y'all find out who be behind these tor-tur-ers?"

"Multumese for asking. I find not, nothing. Naturlich, I think competitor company. I know not which one."

"Ioan, we'all has chillun left in a park in San Remo. Got to be goin' soon-like. Yo'all stay out of trouble. Mebbe Bruno c'n think o' where y'all should hide to."

Bruno nodded enthusiastically. He was eating the richer of the chocolates he'd brought for Ioan. "Multumese for your kindness in coming to see Ioan." He walked us to Ioan's door, and we found our way out through the glorious Garnier building.

Back in San Remo our progress to the park was delayed due to an annual parade of local transvestites. From our rental car's windows we could watch the incredible sight of men dressed in women's clothes of the 1920's and 30's to enter a competition for Flapper styles for transvestites held in front of the city's casino.

No cars were moving. All passengers were rubbernecking exactly as we were.

Most of the transvestites in the competition had exaggerated foam breasts, pushing out the tops of their crazy dresses, totally unlike the *real* styles of want-to-be flat chested girls of the Flapper era.

"Aren't I lucky, Happy darling, I've got a real woman for a wife!"

Happy snuggled closer. There was something different in her snuggle. Was she dreaming of

BEFORE ED? Remembering the halcyon days and nights when I could still make love? Ioan had it tough, losing a leg, having his nose and knuckles broken, yes. But Ioan could *still* plan to make love. I can't.

Chapter 25

When we reached our "chillun" we found they were bored in the park. They'd tried all the swings and roundabouts, and were now inventing their own games. Richard, very pale, wasn't in on the games. He watched closely, perhaps hoping to join in, some day soon.

"Richard, y'all feelin' cold?" Happy, always very solicitous, hugged our youngest and made sure he was the first to pile into our rental car.

I drove beyond the casino. We left behind the competitors for their transvestite Flapper prize. I found a parking bay near a restaurant on the promenade, its wooden plank terrace hanging directly over the nearest beach.

Evening was approaching but an August breeze kept pushing away the few clouds from hiding the last rays of the sun.

Finally I could order the calamari I craved whenever I was in Italy. For the "chillun" we could rely on the local spaghetti. Happy and the babysitter decided to try bowls of minestrone.

A basket of warm breads was plunked down on our table by a messy-haired waitress in jeans and a see-thru T-shirt.

I was peering at her breasts, to make certain they were real and she wasn't another transvestite. when squeals from all three "chillun" broke my concentration.

A bold seagull had joined our party. He flew straight up from the beach to strut on our table top. He pecked at the bread and pulled out a slice, which he promptly threw down to the sand belowplanning to eat it later. Next he tasted meat balls from the spaghetti on our chilluns' plates. They didn't mind. They chirped at him in delight.

Happy shooed the seagull from our table top. She threw more of the bread down to the beach to keep him from the chilluns' food.

This was one very experienced seagull. He'd been plying his tricks since the restaurant had re-opened after the winter's seasonal lull. He'd staked out his territory. We watched as less clever seagulls approached the bread on his territory. Snap went that fearsome bill. Next, a stay-away high pitched screech erupted from him. He fluffed his feathers and scared away the competition like a ghost scaring children at midnight. Proceeding to flirt with my "chillun, he cocked his head and begged like a panhandler outside Covent Garden, using eye-to-eye contact. Our "chillun" loved the bird. They barely ate any meat on their plates, stuffing themselves with the pasta to save all of the meat for their new friend.

"We'all got to buy a bird fo' ourn chillun," Happy exclaimed. "Mebbe one o' them cock-a-tiels wut be real smart like this here cre-a-ture!"

It was difficult to tear away the kids from this cre-a-ture. We had a late train to catch, with two highly inconvenient stops on the route to Paris. We would have to leave the Italian train, climb down one set of stairs and up another at Ventimiglia to get the French train. That, in the middle of the night with the mountain of luggage Happy invariably brought on our travels with the "chillun." In Marseille, we might have to change trains again to get the high-speed three hour express to Paris.

We managed. But our "chillun" were bad-tempered on arrival at the Left Bank hotel Happy had chosen because it was cheap.

The reception area, deserted except for one ancient man wiping at his drowsy eyes, didn't have a sign *Ascenseurs*, which meant we'd have to carry sleepy

Dorothy and sickly Richard up three flights to our rooms. Cranky Tim didn't make things easier with his complaints. The elderly reception clerk handed the keys to us, and I staggered up much-worn steps carrying the luggage. Dorothy perched on my shoulders with her legs wrapped around my neck: her favorite way to travel.

A red light was blinking on the telephone in the master bedroom: our telephone the sole modern convenience in its otherwise Nineteenth Century décor. Oh, no! I punched the green button and heard Merrily's imperious tones.

"To hell with Merrily," I thought: "since Ben bought her colt she's no longer an owner in our stable! How long do I have to put up with her demands?"

There was a letter on the desk, forwarded by our Head Lad from Epsom. It contained news of Lord and Lady Lloyd-Webber's three-time Group 1—winning mare Dar Re Mi being retired from racing. A daughter of Sinspiel, she'd earned 2.7 million pounds in prize money and her wins included the Dubai Sheema Classic and the Yorkshire Oaks, both of which races I knew well because I'd entered mares in them from my stable. The letter's news was that she will travel to visit Oasis Dream in her first covering season. Our Head Lad suggested we follow that example by sending some of Fran's brood mares to Oasis Dream.

Fran continued to be one of the most important owners in my stable. Merrily was just an ex-owner. I ignored the call from Merrily and concentrated on how to pin-point Fran's whereabouts to suggest she send Soviet Gal to Oasis Dream.

There was a telephone number for Fran at the bottom of the letter. I dialed it. To my amazement the call was answered by a receptionist at the Pasteur Institute here in Paris.

Yes, Countess Cabrach could be reached in the patients' wing. Very late for patients to take calls, but yes it was possible to ask her nurse if she would accept one from me.

"Fran? Whom are you visiting at this hour?"

"Visiting! I wish! Rick, I'm undergoing tests for cancer in my throat. Near my vocal chords! I could lose my singing voice. I had an endoscope yesterday. Biopsy. Oh, God. Why me? I never demanded the attention some divas want. I never wanted to be put on a pedestal, idolized, like a pop star. I get my jollies watching horses win, or having great sex."

No filthy swear words tonight.

"Fran! I'm truly sorry you're having such a scare. Happy and I will come to visit you tomorrow morning. We'd planned to take the chunnel train and return to Epsom, but your health is all-important."

"What was the reason for this call?" Blunt, to the point.

"To get your approval to send Soviet Girl to be covered by Oasis Dream. Expensive, but worth it."

"Pay. At this point in my life I need something special to look forward to. When you think you're gravely ill, you don't care about money. Spend it. TIME becomes all-important. I don't want to waste any of it. Please send off Soviet Gal. Happy told me she's in the breeding mood. I want to be alive to see her foal. May have to happen soon."

Fran certainly sounded a different person. Not only there wasn't the usual filthy language, she sounded philosophical.

Her interest in sex hadn't changed.

"Tell me about Ioan. Do you think he'll still be able 'to make the love?'"

"Sure. Even with one leg gone. He hasn't lost his sense of humor. Said he'd do it with a woman who'd lost her right leg to match with his left leg, and they could fit together for 'making the love.'"

"I'd heard he'd lost one leg. Why not both? Is it because Bruno located him in time?"

"Ioan's kidnappers were experts in terror. If Ioan lost both legs and had only the stump of a body, why should he bother revealing the ingredients of the formula they wanted? His lifestyle would be over anyway. So they had *one* leg cut off. The pain, the fear of gangrene. the hopelessness that followed guaranteed their prisoner would tell all rather than have the other leg go too. Clever, devious bastards; those kidnappers. But they didn't guess that Ioan had a sense of humor with-it-all. Ioan gave the ingredients without specifying what amounts should be in the mix. So what he told them guaranteed that any user would grow facial hair."

"Facial hair! But didn't that endanger Ioan further? More torture when the company's experts had experimented with the formula and discovered about the facial hair?"

"Bruno found him in time. Took him to a fellow Romanian's clinic. Ioan's safely in a Romanian goulash. He'll be sent to his native village in Romania's Carpathian Mountains, where his family and the villagers will be as astute at keeping him undercover as the Taliban when hiding hostages in the mountains of Afghanistan."

"Rick, it's so great to hear your voice. Come tomorrow. Bring your Happy." The phone went dead.

Happy was nodding her head. "We'uns sho got to go see Fran in the mornin.' Ah's had thet cancer-scare thing. Po'r woman! Let's usn pray it be nothin'. Like mine were."

After our "chillun" were parked in the Luxembourg Gardens with another babysitter hired through our hotel, we took the Paris Metro to the Pasteur Hospital.

I hate the Paris Metro. Filthy, smelling of urine and full of germs. I recalled reading that Gerard Depardieu had slept there as a homeless teenager. He's very lucky not to have caught TUBERCULOSIS, that I hear is rampant in its stations.

The hospital was located near our stop. We had no difficulty being guided to Fran's room. A semi!

Our pennypinching owner was sharing the room with a woman who coughed incessantly. When I raised my eyebrows in query, Fran reassured me, "That's only a cigarette cough. Stupid cow sneaks in cigarettes on the sly, although she's got cancer of the throat from a lifetime of smoking. Rick, don't frown at me. She can't get upset by what I've said. Doesn't understand English."

"Your friend Ioan seems to be forgetting to speak English. And he's adopted Bruno's awful accent when he *does* try."

"Terrible what those kidnappers did to him. He was such a gorgeous, sexy guy. I *have* found a replacement for him. A Belgian, called Andre Letour.

Smart as a whip. Spent years in the Belgian Congo, now that country's called something else. He never caught anything; no malaria, no leprosy. And I've check it out: no HIV."

Happy kissed her, leaning over the crisp sheets of her upright bed. "How be Jeremy?" she asked bluntly.

"Busy. Jeremy's *always* busy. But he texted to say he'll fly over to Paris with our child if my tests prove positive."

I said nothing. I held out the bouquet of roses I'd brought, although I well knew that Fran had never been thrilled to receive bouquets at the end of her opera performances.

The bouquet got her diverted from starting on the dread topic of her cancer tests.

Fran fiddled with the stem of a rose. "I'm toying with the idea of singing with the Paris Opera. Not as well paid as I'd be at Covent Garden. But I like to encourage new composers, and in Paris they get a better chance of having their works staged. I like operas that have characters you can connect with, like you do with real people."

I suppressed an inappropriate laugh, wondering if Fran meant *vetting* the male singers in the new operas to select one or more as a lover. "Have you got any in mind?"

"Not any of the new singers. But I like some of the directors. The Met's Director, that Peter Sellers person, isn't that new yet I like his work. He calls on you before a performance to ask if you're all right. He has spiky hair and wears odd clothes, but he knows and likes the best new composers. *I* liked working with him. He *breathes* along with you when you're singing, helping you to breathe correctly, which is so important. When I worked with him I felt he knew the opera better than I did, even though I'd been in that role dozens of times before."

Fran's telephone rang. She reached to the night table and listened to Jeremy's voice. Frowning, she certainly didn't have the look of a woman in love with her husband.

Interrupted from giving kudos to the Met's Opera Director, she altered from a pleasant tone to give a disgruntled grunt. She spoke into the telephone as if it would bite her.

"Even if my tests are negative, I won't be going to *her party. Don't say I'm in the Pasteur Hospital. I don't want her to find me. I don't want to talk to her.* I'm not going to lend my name to her guest list to give it free publicity." She hung up. Turning toward Happy, Fran explained, "That was Jeremy to tell me we've been invited by Merrily to a party here in Paris. What a colossal nerve that woman has! No way would I go to any party *she* gives. And it's in such a crazy venue; in an old theater, dating from the 1700s. I suppose she thinks that's a clever idea. Get her more publicity."

I said, "In my youth I was invited by the romance authoress Barbara Cartland to a party in a movie theater to launch one of her new books. She wrote over five hundred, and was always looking for unusual ways to promote her newest. We sat in the regular seats for movie audiences and watched the film version of an earlier book. Then Barbara Cartland went up on stage to say a few words while the screen was replaced by buffet tables offering hot food and quantities of desserts."

"Wut were thet lady like? Ah's read some o' them books," Happy lifted the atmosphere with her chirpy voice and a huge smile.

"Barbara Cartland? Plump, motherly looking. Always wore a bright shade of pink as her image-making color. Very blond hair worn in high wings over her cheeks. Cultured, Oxbridge accent. Always reminded listeners that her brother had been the first officer to die in the World War. Her books? Almost always about a young girl falling in love with an older Duke. Maybe she'd experienced something of the sort herself."

"Rick-honey, ain't you told me thet there were a mess-age from Merrily on ourn hotel te-l-e-phone? Mebbe she be invitin' usn to thet party in a the-a-ter."

"Yes, my darling wife. Spot on. She *did* leave a message inviting us for just exactly that."

"Fo' when?"

"Day after tomorrow."

Fran interrupted. "The results of my tests will be known by then. I'll expect you to bring me home from this hospital, Rick. I may even charter a private plane to get me back to London. There would be enough space for Happy, and those children."

What? Pennypinching Fran charter a plane? I knew that would be a first for her. The offer of helping us out with our "chillun" came as less of a surprise. Hadn't Fran sung for free at our baby Irish's funeral? I'd learned that terrible day that Fran did have a kinder side.

I accepted promptly.

Fran hadn't finished carping about Merrily. "Such a bitch. I can't bear her. But for a moment there I did consider going to her party just to see that teenage-rage BAWDY."

"Bawdy who? Ah's been in Turkey and haven't followed all the careers of those teenage singin' wonders."

"She should be arrested for encouraging child pornography. Bawdy comes on stage to sing her ballads wearing nothing but stamp sized bra and a g-string. In winter she covers that so-called costume with a thick coat, in summer a chiffon mini. Then, like a stripteaser, she casts away the coat and climbs a ladder. She sings from the ladder perched on one leg while kicking her other leg high to show what's between the legs. No voice. Songs are terrible. But Bawdy's albums are outselling everyone's except Madonna's and Lady Gaga's. Now Bawdy's launching her own perfume. She already markets a line of teenage clothes, outselling Banana Republic. Bawdy has also announced she's launching a line of cosmetics and perfumes for teenage girls. And guess who's coming to Merrily's party? BAWDY! It's all over the Paris newspapers. She's hired a private jet to bring her here from *Berlin, where she's been giving sell-out concerts."*

An officious nurse bustled into the room. She fussed over Fran, then politely asked us to leave.

Strolling to the Metro station, Happy started on an unexpected subject. She was dwelling on recent memories. She murmured: "Ah's recallin' them terrible killin's we'all lived through this here year. Them other folks wut died, who weren't so lucky. Hundreds 'n hundreds of folks. Why did they'uns have to die? Ah's been thinkin' thet mebbe them hundreds were killed to cover up the murder o' just one person each time. Who? 'N why? Were them murders related somehow? Were there a serial murd-er-er—killin' them?"

"Hundreds of them, when each time it was to eliminate one person !"

"Somethin' like thet."

We'd arrived at the Metro station, one of the very many serving the fourteen kilometers of the Metro, which in turn served the over twelve million Parisians and the tourists. This particular one was cleaner, perhaps due to its proximity to such a famous cancer hospital.

We got off at the Louvre Station to walk to the Tuilleries, situated on the nearby Seine River. These gardens had been added to since they were begun for a palace in the Sixteenth Century to rival Marie de Medici's Luxembourg Gardens for her chateau on the Left Bank. Neither could claim to be the first public gardens in Paris. That kudo went to Guy de la Brosse, doctor to Louis the Thirteenth, his was planted for medicinal purposes. Happy wasn't interested in its history. She wanted to be rejoined with our "chillun" NOW.

Hugs and kisses followed. I perched Dorothy on my shoulders, locking her tiny legs around my neck and we helped the weary babysitter to collect the two boys from the roundabout.

Tim was in a sneering mood. Using his mother's Kentucky hills accent, he whooped, "Ah's pre-ferred them gardens in San Re-mo."

Chapter 26

For the next two days we dedicated ourselves to the "chillun," outfitting them for winter at the Galeries Lafayette, introducing them to the Guignol puppet shows, and giving each a new haircut, French-style. Happy gave the barber a rocket: "Wut yo'all thinkin' of leavin' hair so messy! New style? Yo'all ain't givin' my chillun nothin' wut could be called a style."

When we'd returned to our room after the unfortunate hair chopping expedition, the red light was blinking furiously at our telephone's base.

Bad news?

No. Very good news.

Fran was on the blower, exulting: "I'm clean. No cancer. The lump in my throat was merely benign. I want you to collect me as soon as possible, Rick.

I want to buy a new outfit, have my hair and nails done, and go to a party. Even Merrily's party!"

Ouch. Happy had listened on the extension and shook her head violently at the words "Merrily's party."

After I'd agreed to escort Fran wherever she wanted to go, my darling wife behaved in an usual-for-her surly way. "Yo'all go with Fran. Ah's goin' to tel-e-phone Maheen t'tell her to come to this here Paris. Only take two hours from Lake Garda. Ah needs her to go do some lookin' with me."

I left in a hurry. No keeping Fran waiting!

Later that evening, Happy filled me in on the results of her "lookin'" with Maheen.

"First off we'uns went t'look at the-a-ters" She loved the Mogador, with its long history. Maheen paid a guide to give them all the background about how Maurice Chevalier, Edith Piaf, and Charles Azvanour had sung in theaters used as concert halls. The guide had produced his i-Phone and played Edith Piaf's JE NE REGRETTE RIEN.

Maheen, very practical, insisted they explore the seedier movie theaters. That done, they'd headed to the Champs Elysees.

The closer the theaters were to the Champs Elysees, the more luxurious they were.

Merrily's party was scheduled to take place later that night at the SUENO Theater. According to Happy it's décor was over-the-top, gawdy. It had a grand entrance, all the frieze work and huge plaster statues concentrated near the one door.

At the SUENO, where frantic preparations for a meal were being rushed ahead following the current film's matinee performance, Happy and Maheen watched while all the seats in the orchestra section were being covered with polyester draperies.

Maheen asked to be shown the CELLAR of this ancient theater. It'd smelled musty.

Happy, always cued by what she'd seen in the movies, remarked that it reminded her of the cellar in PHANTOM OF THE OPERA.

Their new guide pointed out racks of old cans holding films of the Twenties and Thirties. They'd been placed in the Sueno's 'dungeon' during the Nazi Occupation of Paris when even GONE WITH THE WIND was forbidden viewing. Nazi propaganda films had taken the place of Hollywood's best.

The guide pointed at the cans with derision, "Some idiot permitted them to be stored here. Not a good idea. Nitrate film burns three times faster than paper."

Back upstairs, they saw caterers were arriving with huge platters of veal, beef, and sturgeon. The trays of desserts were brought in by a competing caterer, who'd looked angrily at the earlier guys.

Happy pushed Maheen out of the theater before she could nick a chocolate-covered bun from the Saint Honore.

She located a small café nearby and invited Maheen for a coffee at one of its sidewalk tables.

They were quick to down their coffees.

Our "chilluns'" bedrooms were Happy's next stop. With Maheen watching, Happy kissed each sleeping infant, before she joined me in the hotel's downstairs lobby. She asked: "So how did yo'all get along with Fran? She still in-sists on goin' to Merrily's party?" Happy then asked, "Has Jeremy arrived?"

"No. No Jeremy. Still in London at the Lords. As you know, they work into the early hours. I've been ordered to escort her."

"Naw! Rick-honey, yo'all cain't go. Ain't it clear to yo'all thet her the-a-ter's not safe?"

"I've been listening carefully."

"Wut y'all must do, thet be to telephone the fire de-part-ment to get their fire trucks over right now to thet there Sueno The-a-ter."

"Can't do that, my darling. I'd be fined a colossal amount for a false alarm."

"Won't be no false a-larm."

"Darling! You've been brilliant solving past murders, but, murder in a theater full of guests?"

"Y'all must call now. No good fritterin' away val'ble time. Fire engines AND po-lice."

Maheen, who'd stuck as close to Happy as a bandaid on an open sore, added, "Rick, I saw the cans of old films at the Sueno. Happy's right. That stash of old nitrate films will burn so fast it will be a Holocaust in that theater. If you won't make the call, I'll urge Luca to send a text from his police station."

"Yeah, thet be the stuff. 'N Maheen dear, ask Luca to have them Rome po-lice sta-tions to find out wut Merrily were up to when she flew t'It-a-ly. It weren't to help po'r Ioan. She never done nothin' fo' thet man after he lost his laig."

"No good for lovemaking with HER, was what Merrily must have thought!" Bitterly Maheen added, "We need Luca's help. I'm texting him NOW."

We three went upstairs, I opened my bedroom's closet and drew out my dinner jacket and trousers. I fished around for my black tie, and a dress shirt, and cufflinks, then went into the bathroom to change into formal wear and left the girls in the bedroom to wait for Luca's response.

By the time I'd dressed, and re-entered the bedroom, Maheen was looking less baleful.

She said, "Luca's on his way. He's telephoned the top Paris fire department and the Premier District's police. They should arrive at the Sueno Theater on time."

We didn't.

Sharing a taxi with Maheen and Happy, expecting to meet Fran at the Sueno's door, we were still approaching the Sueno when I was astonished to smell putrid fumes and see smoke billowing from a sidestreet off the Champs Elysees.

Our taxi couldn't park anywhere near the Sueno,

It was engulfed in scorching flames. Firemen were hurrying women, clad for an Oscar Night's Red Carpet, out of the scorched soot blackened front entrance.

Happy pointed out the café where earlier she'd given coffee to Maheen. I paid the taxi and we headed for a sidewalk table which had been vacated by a couple coughing badly from the fumes.

Suddenly I began to tremble. Fighting a weakness in my knees, I lurched to the empty table and sank to a chair. I couldn't control an onslaught of shivering. I knew what was causing my troubles: this fire had sparked memories of that ghastly fire at the Palm Beach party when I fought through flames to reach Fran.

Not a safe haven, the café. Some unheeding customers were quarreling over tables, determined to remain in them, regardless.

Rubberneckers, congregating where metal barriers had been set up, were kept at a distance. We had joined the café's customers who were not evacuated.

"Where be Fran?" Happy asked breathlessly.

With difficulty, forcing out each word, I choked, "I told her I'd meet her at the theater. She needed to check into a hotel and change into her new finery."

"And Merrily? No sign o' her!"

Maheen's flat nose swiveled to the opposite direction from the theater. She said, "I think that's Merrily over there, at that other sidewalk café. Take a look."

I did.

Yes, it was Merrily there, squinting rabidly through huge dark glasses in a grotesque effort to recognize the faces of the surviving members of the theater's audience. In a totally absorbed way, she seemed to be waiting.

Waiting for what? Why? The theater was burning to embers. Most of her guests had perished or been hospitalized.

Merrily appeared to be unscathed.

She hadn't volunteered to help. She could have at least provided names of her guests to help in identifying the cadavers.

Instead, just as she had all those many months ago in our cottage in Palm Beach, she sat sipping coffee.

Fran erupted from the Sueno, her hair singed and her new gown blackened from flames. She weaved, and fell into the arms of a fireman. I controlled my shaking legs to rush to help her. Was this going to be a repeat of how the Palm Beach fire ended?

"Have you been badly burned?" I tried to commiserate with her.

Fran's face was reddened from the heat of the embers, but she gasped out, "I'm not burned. It's my vocal chords! My voice . . . The fumes! Don't make me try to speak!" Happy and Maheen hadn't joined us: they were too busy welcoming Luca Palacio, who'd arrived with local police honchos.

Maheen had pushed herself past the metal barriers calling out to Luca. He completed the re-positioning of the barriers to permit Happy and Maheen to join him and the police officers.

"Amore mio," Luca kissed his wife.

Happy, barking in her Kentucky hills accent, ordered, "Arrest thet there woman at the table yonder. She be res-pon-si-ble fo' this fire."

In a calm, steady tone but commanding respect, Luca said, "She's why I'm in Paris. I've come to arrest Merrily Gold for buying potassium chloride on the black market. You should be familiar with potassium chloride, Happy. It's used for executions in the United States to stop the heart."

"Ah knows thet."

"There's a shortage of sodium thiopental, the anesthetic administered as part of a three-dose cocktail along with pancuronium bromide, which paralyzes the muscles. The Rome police believe that Merrily feared there would also be a shortage soon of potassium chloride. Her airplane ride to Rome was to buy enough to kill her next victim."

Luca escorted the two police officers to seize Merrily. She didn't resist arrest. Instead her eyes gleamed with triumph, watching as firemen carried a teenager's corpse to where a pile of body bags loomed.

From the rubberneckers' crowd a hush was followed by shrieks: "That's BAWDY! Our wonderful BAWDY. Poor thing, no coat to cover her g-string and bra now! Burned so bad we can barely know her . . ."

The barriers were broken through. The crowd surged around the teenage corpse. Women wept. Men removed their hats.

From among the men a neatly turned-out professional rushed to Merrily. "Madame Gold, I am a lawyer. I will represent you for whatever crime these outrageous policemen have accused you of. I am famous for arguing before judges how an analysis can go beyond experts' mandate. I will gain your freedom in no time."

"Nah. Thet yo'all WON'T be doin'." Happy gave the man a shove as if he was a rogue horse in a stall at our stables. "Ah's here to make sho' nothin' like thet happens. After we'uns give a proper wake fo' them folks wut died, Ah's goin' in front o' some judge myself to tell the Merrily sto-ry."

I didn't want to wait to hear what Happy would be telling the judge at Merrily's trial. It was my duty to take Fran to the Pasteur Hospital, which was where she wanted to go. We were escorted through the open barriers. A policeman hailed a taxi for us. To relieve her trembling, and to stop her from going into shock, I removed my dinner jacket to cover Fran's singed bare shoulders.

Why the Pasteur? The great hospital for treating cancer! This night, in her terror, Fran felt it would be a home away from home.

We found a doctor there on night duty who recognized Fran as having been a patient earlier that day. She was returned to her semi, given warm food and wrapped in blankets. Medications were provided for her vocal cords. Shortly before midnight I could finally head for my hotel.

In our Paris suburb, in that hotel's kingsize bed, I held Happy in my arms while she spelled out how she'd come to know that Merrily was a serial killer. The subject was horrific, but the deep comfort I felt with my Happy cuddled beside me was enough to finally calm my own nightmare memories of the two fires.

Happy kissed me for a long time. When my renewed shivering finally ceased, she began. "Ah's known fo' some time thet Merrily be a serial killer."

"How?"

"It began to niggle at me in thet there Palm Beach, when we'all went to see thet house wut burned down. Ah found somethin' sus-pi-cious at the sign used by them valet parkin' boys. Y'all re-mem-bers? Someone had tossed away a wax-covered pine cone left over from a cache of fire-lighters."

"A firelighter! Could it have Merrily's DNA on it?"

"Ah'd bet it do. Fo' the next murders, Merrily needed pro-fess-ion-al help. She got a explo-sive expert. One who'd know how to o-per-ate a roadside bomb. Dynamited the car Merrily had suggested to Jasmine thet she use. Po'r driver, 'n the passengers o' both the cars in front. All died. Same explosive expert must've thrown the grenade wut hit the gas pipes of Merrily's' Chelsea building wut exploded with all them cosmetic company competitors and her own executives blown to bits."

"But she LIKED Jasmine. And why on earth would Merrily blow up her building and kill so many of her own cosmetics executives?"

"Yeah. Liked her until Jasmine started to climb too high on the ladder toward the chairmanship 'n mebbe give Merrily the push. The Chelsea buildin' weren't impo'tant to Merrily. Insured, anyhows. Her executives? Easy to replace in this here De-press-ion. Wut Merrily did was to wipe out a whole gen-er-a-tion of future com-pe-ti-tors in the cos-met-ics industry. Specially them ones she'd met at thet con-ven-tion in Monte Carlo. Thet didn't in-clude Ioan, he weren't invited to thet party. Sure not. He knew the secret formula of his company's no-wrinkles cream. Merrily had other plans fo' him!"

"Yes, to have thugs break his knuckles and his nose if he wouldn't give them the formula."

"Yo'all knows them two kidnappers are in thet pro-vin-cial jail in Turkey. Very un-pleasant ex-per-ience fo' them. Remember the movie MIDNIGHT EXPRESS wut shows wut it be like in a Turkish jail? Ah'll make an-other bet, thet after a month o' jailtime them two will tell a judge thet Merrily sent them to do thet job."

Happy appeared to have rethought her opinion of Ioan. Like the New York stock market, his stock went up and down. Up, when she met him and he escorted her gallantly to her seat in Covent Gardens' Opera House. Down, when Happy learned of the rough sex tricks he'd used on Basha. Up again when she observed that he hadn't lost his sense of humor after losing a leg in Italy.

I went back to the subject of the two British thugs. "Locked up, they couldn't have pulled off tonight's holocaust."

"Naw. Ah reckons like when Merrily were in Rome buyin' poison on the Black Market, she done made a Si-ci-lian Mafia connection. Them Si-ci-lians be special a-dept at settin' fires. Mafia guy could have passed hisself off as one of the caterers' waiters, gone to the cellar, opened the cans of nitrate film, lit an oily rag near them, threw away his waiter's towel and joined the members of the matinee audience strollin' from the the-a-ter."

"Happy darling, I read somewhere that in the United States it's a serious charge to be in a conspiracy to kill in a foreign country. You might get Merrily charged with conspiracy to kill thanks to your saving the pin from the grenade launched at her building's party. That, in case her DNA has been wiped from the firelighter."

My precious wife sighed. Wishing for more than a cuddle?

I wasn't to know. She changed the subject. "Yo'all think Fran will still give usn a ride to London in a pri-vate jet?"

"Yes. She'll hire a jet to take all of us back to England. Jeremy called to say he'd be at the Pasteur Hospital shortly. He's bringing their baby son on the late chunnel train. He believes Fran's problem isn't physical. She's hurting psychologically. She's so afraid the blaze's smoke has injured her vocal cords, she doesn't dare to speak much and discover they're all right."

"Like when Ah was in Ire-land 'n thought that Richard were bein' born when he weren't quite ready."

"Something similar. The plane is chartered for three p.m. tomorrow afternoon. We'll check out of this hotel and hope."

By two in the afternoon the following day Happy had packed all of that mountain of "chillun" clothes that she travels with when we've got the three on board. She hadn't bought a single Paris treat for herself. The Duty Free in the airport for chartered planes had nothing as fine as she would have found at similar shops in the Orly or Charles De Gaulle Airports. But I sneaked a bottle of Chanel Number Five—not WOW!Me—with a fast pass with my credit card in the small airport's shop.

Duty free? Not quite!

We'd removed our shoes in Security, the bell had rung because I had my keys in a pocket, when Fran appeared with Jeremy and their baby. She looked rested. She seemed comforted by her family being with her. How long would that last?

Our Richard and their baby boy were fast friends, They'd seen a lot of each other because Richard had shared his toys with the boy.

Dorothy and Tim had to make do with the toys distributed by the one stewardess. Tim demanded to go up front to the pilots' cabin, and he got his way! I'm going to have to curb his imperious manners.

Jeremy and Fran were plumbing Happy's inside knowledge of the WOW!Me story. They wanted to know how Merrily had made so much money, and why she'd been so determined to add an extra billion to her company's revenue.

Drinks were passed to us by the stewardess.

Champagne.

I guessed that would loosen up my Happy. She had a clairvoyanat's powers, but could barely hold her own after a flute of champagne.

"Don't know as Ah's right about it all, but Ah's sho given Merrily's killin's plenty o' thought. In Palm Beach, she'd took Rick upstairs, 'n next day Ah's wanted to see her bedroom too. When she done showed me her bedroom and Ah's seen wut a mess it were with packages of cosmetics and bottles of per-fume all over ever' avail'ble space, even on top o' her bed leavin' only a few inches fo' her to sleep, Ah'd begun to wonder wut-all made her tick."

"Money."

"Yeah, but it were mo'e like fo' wut folks calls am-bi-tion. She poisoned huh first husband, a Alabama farmer, to own his proper'ty 'n sell it fo' to get her a stake fo' to start a bu'ness. Then she went 'n married an E-gypt-ian who owned a cache of musk fo' makin' per-fume thet lasts."

"Murdered her first husband!"

"Sho thing. Merrily weren't no Holly Golightly in BREAKFAST AT TIFFANY'S who, bein' a big call-gal in Noo York, sent off her farmer husband to a bus station to get him out o' town. Naw. Ah reckons as Merrily used a simple old poison like tinc-ture from Oleanders, as we makes to kill roaches in Kentucky."

"Good grief! Musk. Secreted by male deer used as a basis for perfumes. How would a farmer's wife from Alabama get to know about musk? And meet an Egyption with a lot of the stuff?"

"Weren't easy. Accordin' to Jasmine, it took Merrily some doin' with many many men befo'e she got out o' Al-a-bama. Probably like wut Evita had to do when she got to Bu-e-nos Ai-res in the movie called fo' her. Met the E-gyptian in Noo York, where one guy had dumped her. Had to give a baby son to thet E-gypt-ian befo'e he parted with his stash o' musk. But thet E-gypt-ian. He guessed Merrily's game, so he done survived. Not poisoned.

Went home to E-gypt. Them E-gypt-ians knows plenty about poison. Didn't yo'all see the movie with Elizabeth Taylor about CLE-O-PATRA and how she done poisoned herself with an adder's bite?"

Movies! It had often seemed to me that my darling Happy's education depended in great part thanks to the old films she'd watched on Turner Classic Movies. I asked her, "Hap, how did Merrily get into cosmetics, in addition to perfume?"

"By mo'e climbin'. Seen how other big names in the Beauty Bus-i-ness added to their fo'tunes. Some, like Helena Rubinstein, had started with cosmetics, then added perfumes."

Fran's chartered jet was flying over Windsor Castle. Such a grand sight to jolt an Englishman's heart. I pointed it out to Dorothy, and she clapped her hands.

We had lots of goodbyes after landing. Hurrying through the rain to the terminal, I wondered how long it would be until we saw Fran again.

Chapter 27

Not long. Fran came to see us at our Epsom stables with her hyper-active son. After checking on our fillies, Fran wanted young Peregrine to sit on Tim's pony.

"Shucks, Fran. We'all loves yourn little boy. But Ah don't want nothin' bad to happen to him like wut killed Bonnie Blue, the daughter o' Scarlett 'n Rhett in GONE WITH THE WIND."

Gentling her voice, Fran said quietly, "But you are here, Hap. YOU know how to control a pony."

Sighing. Happy acted on Fran's order to give Peregrine a leg-up, jockey style, and walked the pony around our stableyard with that valuable infant on board.

"Next yo'all will be takin' him over jumps,. Not until he be four, at least," Happy called out, lest Fran bought her heir a pony of his own for the Cabrachs' castle grounds.

Peregrine, very forward for his age, could hold the reins competently, had an excellent seat in the saddle, and showed definite promise as a jockey. Woe for the Cabrachs, if the next Earl wanted that job. I remembered well how Britain's Royal Family kept their opinions private when first HRH Princess Anne got her jockey's license and proceeded to win races competing against top professionals. And then how HRH Prince Charles, its heir as Prince of Wales, proceeded to take part against the jump horses' pros, coming in Second on his own horse at Ludlow Race Course.

As trainer to Fran's fillies, I couldn't bad mouth the idea of encouraging Peregrine's love of horses. I did feel very relieved when Timmy replaced Peregrine on our pony. Tim, who had no love of horses of any sort, never raced or tried to jump the pony. He was demonstrating his customary selfishness. Immediately after Fran collected Peregrine, Tim was ultra quick to finish his stint in the stableyard.

That night, after Fran left with Peregrine for their castle, Happy astounded me with an untimely suggestion.

She asked me if she could borrow our Volvo to go North to the autism center where Merrily's son was confined.

"My darling Happy, take the car. But I know that big heart of yours, and I hope you're not planning to take over the care of Merrily's boy. He's thirteen, a difficultt age in any boy's life. With an adolescent suffering from Autism, forget it! And we haven't any money to help someone else's son. Little Richard's condition may bankrupt us, and we have got to think of him, first."

"Ah always thinks o' ourn chillun. First be y'all. Then, our chillun. But Rick, thet don't mean as Ah's got to stop helpin' other folks. This boy, he ain't got nobody. It's mostly my fault his Ma's goin' to prison fo' life, o' to thet there Al-a-bama 'lectric chair."

"So, you've got a guilt complex. Is that it?"

"Naw. Merrily be one o' the worst killers Ah's had to corner. Worst, 'cause Merrily done killed so many other people most times she wanted to get rid of someone. Her boy? Ah's just got to see wut Ah c'n do!"

Happy, as always, got her way. She asked so seldom for favors. Now she revved the engine and grinded the gears. No good. She couldn't get the Volvo up our manure-slippery driveway. I got in the driver's seat, she trudged behind the car to our level road, and there I hugged her, "Safe trip!" I said, No way did I play the hypocrite choraling, "Have a good trip!" I knew that Rafiq's "free" institution would be grim. Much worse than Anya's expensive "place."

Chapter 28

Happy had done her homework. As a fan of Google, she'd honed up on Autism.

Soon she'd nosed our Volvo past the institution's dreaded gates. They were bordered on either side by wires that could electrocute a child trying to escape. We'd had similar when I tried to raise cattle, and needed electric wire to box in the cattle.

Happy had already had her anbitions for this boy written in stone in her mind. Happy's homework had suggested that children with Autism could show significant improvement when given 400 mgs of carnosine twice a day for eight weeks. Carnosine, being an amino acid could enhance the function in the frontal lobe of the children's brains.

Carnosine had a ninety percent success rate. Children with severe Autism sometimes were able to talk better, had more cognitive function, their epileptic fits came less often, and they could think more clearly then mix more normally with other children.

"But will I be able to afford to buy thet carnosine?" Happy asked herself, as she found her way to the institute's head bosswoman.

Happy had prepared a list of questions for the woman. But when she saw the ogre who sat across from her at the center's reception desk, Happy abandoned any thought of facing down the Superintendant.

"May Ah see Merrily Gold's son, please?" she asked, as carefully as a lamb might bleat in a lion's cage, "Ah's been with his Mom last week."

"Would that be the week the woman was arrested for buying poison on the Black Market in Italy? Or the week she killed hundreds of her guests in a theater in Paris?" The woman's face became uglier. Her downturned slit of a mouth was wet in its corners as if she was salivating with a putrid sense of humor over Merrily's evil doings.

"The boy. Ah's come fo' the son."

"We'd be only too glad to turn him over to you. But that's not possible without a court order."

Happy knew when she was bested. "May Ah go see him, anyways?"

The woman shrugged. She sent glances quickly to the four corridors leading to this reception area. With no one approaching, she pointed to a bleak yard beyond the left corridor.

Not wasting a second, Happy dashed to the door that led to the yard. There, she had to deal with a child-safe key. No chances taken in this institution. Happy felt she really could have been entering a lion's cage.

Once inside the yard Happy saw that most of the children were younger than thirteen. Happy found only one adolescent. He sat crouched like a cat in a kennel of dogs. She went over to him and offered some of the awful hushpuppies she'd cooked for the boy.

He swiped at them, his right hand like a manatee's flipper. Chewing, he spat out one after the other. He changed his sitting position to rest his knees and elbows on the yard's dirt surface.

Happy behaved as if she was in her pastor's rectory at a church supper. "Hi, yo'all. My name's Hillary, but folks call me lil ole Happy. Sorry Ah didn't make them hushpuppies mo'e tasty. Next time when Ah comes t'see yo'all, Ah could bring better."

"Gingersnaps," the boy said clearly. "Ah wants me some gingersnaps." He'd recognized a regional

American accent, and that had prompted him to speak. "Y'all from Al'bama?"

His accent was stronger than Happy's.

"Nah. Ken-tuck. No'th o' the Mason Dixon line. We'uns got the best hosses. Yo'all like hosses?" She dangled that information like a charm for a trinket bracelet.

Nod, and the beginnings of a smile.

"My husband, Rick, he be a trainer o' racehosses. We got some mighty purty ones. If yo'all come to live with usn, Ah'd let yo'all ride one thet be right gentle."

"Promise?"

Happy nodded. "Honest injun, cross my heart 'n hope to die. When Ah pro mises, Ah keeps my promises." Happy looked down at the boy's shoes. They were too short, too small for his feet. She eased off his shoes. His socks were too small too, forcing his toes to curl. "Step on my piece o' paper 'n Ah'll draw me the size o' yourn foot. Next time Ah's goin' to bring yo'all shoes 'n socks wut fit."

His shoes and socks not only didn't fit, they were filthy and very worn. No one had provided him with shoes or socks for a very long time.

"Next week?"

"Ah promise. Even if'n Ah cain't get the cou't order Ah needs t'take yo'all home with me as soon as Ah'd like. Bye fo' now." Happy kept their meeting brief.

In the late evening, when she'd arrived back home at our stables, Happy told me what she thought of the situation.

"Rick, Ah thinks thet Merrily ain't done nothin' fo' thet boy except carry him in her stomach 'n birth him. Ah's learned me thet his name be Rafiq Hassan. He be fou'teen, not thirteen. His jacket were fo' a boy o' ten. He'd like to come to live where there be hosses."

"We can't afford that luxury. Sorry, Happy darling. And he could prove to be dangerous for our "chillun." Hurt Dorothy, playing too rough, or worse. Rape her! We mustn't forget his mother's a killer. And God only knows what MISTER Hassan was mixed up with, in addition to having a stash of musk. Maybe drugs."

"Ah doesn't b'lieve thet evil folks have evil chillun less'n the chillun done lived with their folks 'n learned them their evil ways. Honest injun, ain't necess-a-sarily so. Rafiq, he ain't never lived with Merrily, nor with thet Hassan man."

We went upstairs to our useless kingsize bed, and I got a hot water bottle for Happy. Sad, but it was the best I could do for her that night. I let her pull most of the covers over to her side of the bed, while I plotted how to keep Rafiq out of our home.

I didn't succeed. Rafiq duly arrived and came to live in our attic bedroom with his pathetic bag of poor rubbish. No pajamas. No toothbrush. No slippers. No sweater. Two shirts, one still unwashed.

His one set of trousers and jacket, just as Happy had described, were for a ten-year-old boy and long ago outgrown.

Was he autistic? Or misdiagnosed as Anya had been? Could he have been faking, for good reason?

Happy had Googled autism and read up on the newest treatments for it in the public library's medical encycloepedia.

We planned to test his condition at home, but not before taking him to London on our monthly trip to Richard's Addison's Disease doctor for a referral to a specialist there in Autism to get a professional opinion. No, Rafiq didn't have an impairment to his limbic brainstem pathways. No, Rafic didn't have a liver detoxification problem. No, there wasn't any damage to the development to the limbic and subfrontal systems of the brain. Yes, Rafiq had a leaky gut. And that Happy could deal with, or so she believed.

"Doc, do yo'all think as Ah could mebbe fix his damaged gut?"

"Mrs. Harrow, the protocol today is very different from what we suggested only a year ago. Clinical prevention is changing both constantly and rapidly. There is no question but that with our present understanding of Autism, biochemistry, toxicology,neurology, physiology, and clinical presentation you could probably do as much good for Rafiq as any of us here."

"'N where-all does Ah begin?"

"My professional advice would be to start with digestive enzyme supplements."

"Be they awful expensive-like? We ain't got much money to spend."

"I understand. You two Harrows already have the burden of an Addison's Diseased child. But with Rafiq, IF he has Austism, and I couldn't be sure of that after having examined him as thoroughly as time permitted, you could start by dipeptidyl-peptidase 4, which is casoglutenase, to break down the undesirable morphine-like peptides from casein and gluten."

"Wut? This here boy Rafiq got him somethin' like a morphine addict might?"

"You could say that. With Autism, we simply can't be certain of whatever we say. For instance, we sometimes recommend friendly bacteria to eliminate gastrointestinal pathogens. A gastrointestinal problem could have resulted in a change in his gut environment and an imbalance in the normal bacterial flora. Overgrowths of yeast, parasites, and undesirable anaerobic bacteria occur. The bad organisms not only affect digestion negatively but also produce toxic substances such as alcohols and aldehydes. You can try administering to Rafiq a bouquet of herbs, and an antiobiotic. But, dear lady, I personally recommend overwhelming the bad bacteria with good bacteria. Give Rafiq large doses of good bacteria such as acidophilus, lactobacillus and some soil-based organisms which could adhere to the gut wall. Believe it or not, these given in daily doses should prodce over one hundred million organisms."

I interrupted all this medical palaver. "Are you suggesting yoghurt? Our kids love the low-fat kind with different fruit flavors."

"Perhaps not the commercial kind. But real yoghurt, most certainly. The acidopholus is just what he needs. And vitamins, with added minerals. Just be sure   that Rafiq gets some sulphur daily. Almost every autistic child is deficient in sulphur. However, orally administered sulphates will feed the bad bacteria and fungi, causing a bloom of bad organisms and a worsening of autistic systems. I recommend that sulphate and magnesidum be administered through the skin. For instance, you could add a cup of Epsom salts to his bathwater."

Happy, who'd been holding her breath, now exhaled.

"Sho 'nuf, Epsom salts in Rafiq's bath water. Ah c'n do thet all right."

We left the specialist's white-tiled office in an atmosphere of positive expectations. Yoghurt? Epsom salts in bathwater? Those my Happy could understand and implement.

In her Kentucky hills the locals had used those from time immemorial.

At home, Rafiq took to following us on our morning and evening gallops. He'd run alongside us at gallops as far as he could manage.

On the regular day that Happy entertained a group of children in the Riding For The Handicapped-program, Rafiq's eyes glowed with a fresh interest.

"Me too," he announced, getting in line to wait with the handicapped children for a chance to ride.

Rafiq had a surprisingly good seat on a horse. He slouched with a curved spine when walking or running. But he was straight as an arrow on horseback.

His mount recognized this boy was sick. In the intuitive way that some horses have, this mount knew he had to be gentle and not cause trouble.

Over the following weeks Rafiq spent most of his daytime hours in our stables. The nights were still long in September, and he could wait for us through evening stables. He found an extra bucket and took to cleaning horse manure from the stalls. Eventually, he learned the right quantity of food to put in hay racks. He mixed in the proper extras to complete our horses' diets.

His favorite moment came when he was permitted to give an apple or carrot to his mount.

With nights growing longer and our days shorter, he would stare long at the ivy growing red on stable walls. He'd never seen anything like that in Alabama.

Rafiq started in the nearest school, dropped in with younger kids, but very comforted not to be with Autistic children.

On the first evening of autumn, holding her in my arms, cuddling, in our useless kingsize bed, I asked Happy HOW she'd performed this miracle. "Like the nurse did in the story of Helen Keller in the old TV film "The Miracle Continued?""

"Nah! Don't give me no credit. Weren't no miracle. Were just by talkin' to Rafiq, 'n listenin' to him. He done told me his story. It were wut Ah'd ex-pect-ed. Rafiq done told me thet his Ma killed a farmer, Rafiq seen her cut him up with a kit-ch'n knife."

"And I'll guess that Merrily KNEW he'd seen. That's why he was kept at the farm the Egyptian had bought for Merrily. Kept there to live with a farmhand."

"Yeah. No schoolin'. No good food. Scraps from the farmhand's grits 'n hushpuppies. No veg. No fruits. No cow on the farm, so no milk. Shoes always sizes too small. Has hammer toes from thet."

"Does he know what his mother did to dispose of the farmer's body?"

"The farmhand done seen him dump it inro the Gulf. So Merrily rode her truck over the farmhand, left him paralyzed. Brain useless. To protect hisself, Rafiq pretended t'be stupid, 'n un-able t'speak from shock. Without the farmhand t'feed and babysit Rafiq, Merrily sent her son to a place fo' autistic kids. Docs there plenty pleased t'take her money."

"But, my darling, I'll bet that Merrily sent him to the free place in England, as soon as she found out that was viable."

"Not takin' no bets on thet! Merrily never spent no cash on her boy lessen it were t'pro-tect herself. 'N now be too late. Merrily done be broke. Wut with the families of all them hundreds of folks she killed suin' her."

"Those families are entitled to every last penny So it's just as well that Rafiq has no ambition to go to Oxford. He wants to be a groom, caring for racehorses. And as long as I train, he'll have a place in our stables."

"He done told me thet at his Ma's farm, his only pal were the old grey mare there. Now he's got ourn million-dollar racehosses to love. Rafiq even done learned him how to make them squares on a mare's back fo' the hide t'look purty when they'uns goes to a racetrack. 'N thet ain't easy. Wut with gettin' the brushin' right."

The days grew shorter. October was soon on us: that sublime month of harvest time and the time for one of my favorite races: The Queen Elizabeth II Stakes at Ascot.

To prepare Rafiq for the day of racing at Ascot, I dug out some of the DVDs from my collection of old racehorse films. We screened "National Velvet" with the twelve-year-old Elizabeth Taylor, and "The Black Stallion" with an aging Mickey Rooney. For a newer film I showed him "Seabiscuit."

On the morning of that Ascot race Happy took Rafiq shopping for a new blazer that fit and trousers that were properly down to his ankles. She bought a very simple felt hat for herself, a hat fit for a trainer's wife, not a fanciful concoction.

We left the "chillun" at home with Amah, because they were still under the age when I felt they could enjoy a day's racing.

Driving past fields with the "stalking" of wheat sheaves in machine made huge rolls, unlike my old-fashioned preferred way of bunching wheat stalks vertically, I gloried in the autumn colors. There was the yellow-gold of the wheat, the green of lettuce, the red from changing leaves. Wonderful!

Rafiq asked me twice whether his mother would be electrocuted by Yellow Mama when she was extradicted to Alabama. "Sent back home," was how he put it.

For á few minutes I tapped my ear, insinuating I couldn't catch what he was asking over the racket made by my old car's engine. I wanted to give considerable thought to what answer I should give to this overly-sensitive boy, I felt I had to reply to his third query, but needed time to do that properly.

I leaned my ear close to his lips, and then spoke with feeling, "Not sure, Raf. Maybe," I said, "I know she's going to be on Death Row. I won't lie to you about that. But Happy wrote to Alabama police to check on the blood they found in Merrily's farmhouse bedroom. It was the farmer's blood. In Alabama, there are murders for which prosecutors demand the death penalty by electrocution. In Alabama that does mean by Yellow Mama."

My darling wife attempted to ease the bad news with some good news. "When Merrily's es-tate were put under scru-ti-ny it were dis-co-vered thet Merrily done ap-pro-priated a stash o' the musk yourn father kept in storage. Legally, it were yourn father's. It be yourn now. Val-uable!"

Happy added: "From thet musk yo'all will have 'nuf money fo' t'have a coll-ege ed-u-ca-tion. Or some day t'buy a little house o' yourn own."

"Ah's don't wants to go to no college. Ah's don't wants no house. Ah's wants t'stay with y'all."

"Sho nuf. Still, it be right nice t'have some money o' yourn own." Happy winked at Rafiq. "Ah's goin' t'screen thet movie THE PRINCE AND THE PAUPER fo' yo'all 'n learn yo'all how nice it be to go from a pauper t'be a prince. 'N y'all c'n stay a prince."

I had some news to add. "Rafiq, I don't know if you ever learned that your mother had built up a billion dollar company after she left Alabama."

"Naw. Ah's never been tol' nothin' like thet."

"It was called WOW!Me. It made lipstick, perfume, and face creams. But the pure Foods and Drugs Administration learnedf that there were traces of addict-makng cocaine in the lipsticks. The whole company was closed down and has now gone bankrupt. That means it no longer exists. All WOW!Me products have been recalled worldwide."

Happy perked up. "Didn't Ah hear me thet first day thet the lipstick had cocaine in it?"

"Yes, my darling wife, you did." My wife really is a wonder.

Our Volvo entered Ascot's High Street. There was no formidable queue to enter the racecourse or carparks which would have been the case for Royal Ascot races.

We kept going at twenty kilometers an hour to reach the Owners and Trainers carpark. It was still shaded by fat trees that had not cast their leaves. I raised my hat to a former neighbor, Richard Hannon, and congratulated him for being leading trainer. Together we walked to the Trainers' stand.

Thank God for Admiral's Barge. That great old gentleman performed as he had so often before. How that horse loved the Ascot course's gradients! I waited until after the first race to check on Fran's filly: Soviet Flower. A two-year-old, I hadn't raced her yet this year because I didn't like to give two-year-old fillies early runs.

Soviet Flower looked well and ready to do her business. On her toes and with ears pricked she paraded in the ring and gave me reason to hope she could win. Fran hadn't come because Jeremy was due to give a speech, about M15's activities, later in the afternoon in the House of Lords.

No stress due to any eyeball-to-eyeball demands from Fran! The demands had come to me by e-mail, which I'd digested in good heart in my tack room-cum-office. As the horses circled the paddock I could enjoy that sublime sight.

The Monarch does not always attend the race which had been named for her. On this day the Royal Box had been spruced up with autumn flowers and she could be seen through its safety glass to enthusiastically encourage the weight for age horses in their race.

The Monarch had attended on that day because she had a favored two-year-old filly in the same race as Soviet Flower.

Like she had as a young girl, Queen Elizabeth jumped with glee when her filly came in Second. Her Majesty knew that Second for a two-year-old means "knocking on the door" to win in her three-year-old-season.

Our entry, Soviet Flower, had taken the race. And, joy! The Monarch, such a good sport, came down to the ring to present the small trophy. It was my privilege to receive it, because Fran was absent.

I did my short-neck bow and thanked Queen Elizabeth.

Happy brought Rafiq to share in the presentation.

Her Majesty recognized Happy and, as on earlier occasions when Happy had recently added a child to our family, the Monarch flashed her smile and said in her cut-glass accent: "Mrs. Harrow, I didn't know you had a teenage son."

"Oh, yes Ma'am. We done adopted—Ah means—we adopted this one recent-like."

Queen Elizabeth turned to Rafiq. "And what is your name, young man?"

Surprise! Rafiq copied my short-neck bow, said Ma'am properly as he'd heard it from Happy, and replied, "Ma'am, Ah's called Rafiq."

The Queen nodded, her smile widened, and then HM swiveled to face our jockey to praise him for his ride. Rafiq's grand moment was over, but the afterglow shone all over his eugenically-tanned face.

We remained in the Trainers' stand to watch that most glorious of England's autumn races, The Queen Elizabeth II Stakes. I'd first seen it as a boy when that very successful breeder, Lord Rotherwick, had the honor of winning with Homing. On another occasion I'd seen Paris-based American George Strawbridge's colt win it. On this day we left shortly after that race.

We had another drive ahead of us the following morning.

Isn't life wonderful!

-000-